THE PROPHETIC VISION
OF JAMES BLISH'S
SCIENCE FICTION

"One of the few masters of this mode who has fused with his power-driven imagination an incandescent style is James Blish . . . his galactic series of novels, "Cities in Flight," have probably carried the concept of space travel a multiplicity of light years further than anyone has been able to contemplate."

The London Times Literary Supplement

Once in a great while, a really new idea comes along in science fiction. In his epic series James Blish structures an entire universe in which mankind is no longer bound to earth and becomes both conquerer and victim of the stars.

In A LIFE FOR THE STARS James Blish hurtles the reader into the fantastic world of spindizzy fields and anti-death pills as earth's cities one by one leave the tired and dying planet to find new wealth among unknown stars.

JAMES BLISH'S FAMOUS *Cities in Flight* NOVELS

I THEY SHALL HAVE STARS

"His climax, when humanity out-
wits its human tormentors and es-
capes forever from the vicious rat-
race which they have created, is
extraordinarily effective."

—*The Oxford Times*

II A LIFE FOR THE STARS

This highly imaginative story of the
future tells how whole cities abandon the world to wander in space.

III EARTHMAN, COME HOME

"This is a good picaresque novel,
and excellent SF, for the more one
knows of scientific principles the
deeper one's appreciation of Blish's
resourcefulness."

—*Brian Aldiss*

IV THE TRIUMPH OF TIME

"Both characters and moral problems have been brought brilliantly
to life in the weird yet coherent universe of Mr. Blish's imagination."

—*The Sunday Times*

A LIFE FOR THE STARS

James Blish

AN AVON BOOK

To L. Sprague DeCamp

AVON BOOKS
A division of
The Hearst Corporation
959 Eighth Avenue
New York, New York 10019

First Avon Printing, October, 1963
Third Avon Printing, May, 1966

Cover photo by Lida Moser

Printed in Canada

CONTENTS

A LIFE FOR THE STARS

1

PRESS GANG

From the embankment of the long-abandoned Erie-Lackawanna-Pennsylvania Railroad, Chris sat silently watching the city of Scranton, Pennsylvania, preparing to take off, and sucked meditatively upon the red and white clover around him.

It was a first time for each of them. Chris had known since he had been a boy—he was sixteen now—that the cities were deserting the Earth, but he had never seen one in flight. Few people had, for the nomad cities, once gone, were gone for good.

Nor was it a very happy occasion, interesting though it was. Scranton was the only city Chris had ever seen, let alone visted, and the only one he was ever likely to see. It represented what small livelihood his father and his older brother had been able to scratch out of this valley; it was where the money was made, and where it was spent, somehow always managing to go out faster than it came in.

Scranton had become steadily greedier as the money to be made dwindled, but somehow never greedy enough. Now, as it had for so many other towns, the hour of the city's desperation had struck. It was going into space, to become a migrant worker among the stars.

The valley sweltered in the mercilessly hot July sunlight, and the smoke from the plant chimneys rose straight up. There were only a few smokestacks going, though, and those would be shut down shortly, until the city should find another planet on which to work. Nothing would be allowed to smoke in the confined air of a star-cruising vessel, even as big a one as a city—not so much as a cigarette.

Down at the bottom of the railroad embankment, where the tar-paper shacks huddled, a red-necked man in an undershirt and levis scratched at a kitchen garden with a hoe. Chris wondered if he knew what was about to happen. Certainly he was paying no attention; maybe he just didn't care. Chris's own father had reached the gloomy state of mind long ago. But all the same, it was odd that there were no sight-seers other than Chris himself.

A circular belt of cleared land, nothing but raw, red, dry earth, ran around the city, separating it from the shacks, from the battered and flaking suburbs, and from all the rest of the world. Inside it, the city looked the same as always, even to the yellow and orange glare of the slag heaps. Scranton was going to leave half its homes behind, but it was taking the slag heaps along; they were part of its stock in trade. Somewhere, out among the stars, there would be a frontier planet with iron ore to process; somewhere else, a planet with a use for slag, or something that might be extracted from slag —a use still beyond speculation, but not to be fore-closed by shortsightedness. People, on the other hand, were largely useless; weight for weight, the slag would be worth more.

At least, that was the hope. What was certain was that there was no more iron ore on Earth worth process-ing. The voracious Second Millennium—the books called it the "Age of Waste"—had used it all up, except for such artificial mines as used-car dumps and other de-posits of scrap and rust. There was still native iron on Mars, of course, but none of that was available for

10

Scranton. Pittsburgh was already on Mars, as well equipped with guns as with blast furnaces. Besides, Mars was too small a planet to support more than one steel town, not because the red world was short of iron, but because it was short of oxygen, which was also essential for the making of steel.

Any work Scranton might find to do now would have to lie beyond the reaches of the solar system. There was no iron on Venus or Mercury that a steel town could afford to process—and no iron at all on the other six planets, the five gas giants and the remote ice ball that was Pluto.

The man in the kitchen garden straightened, leaned his hoe against the back of his shack, and went inside. Now the valley outside the raw-earth circle looked deserted indeed, and it suddenly occurred to Chris that this might be more than an appearance. Was there something dangerous about being too close to a city under a spindizzy field? Were he and the lone gardener being foolhardy?

At the moment, the whole world was silent except for the distant grumbling of Scranton itself. He knew he had nothing to fear from the rail bed behind him, for the tracks had been torn up long ago to feed the furnaces. There was a legend in the valley that on quiet nights one could still hear the Phoebe Snow going by, but Chris scoffed at such fairy tales. (Besides, his father had told him, that had been a daytime train.) Even the ties were gone, burned as firewood by the shack dwellers through generations of harsh Pennsylvania winters.

He racked his memory for what little he knew about the behavior of spindizzies, but could come up with nothing but that they were machines and that they lifted things. Though his schooling had been poor and spasmodic, he was a compulsive reader, devouring even the labels on cans if there was nothing else available; but the physics of interstellar flight is an impossible discipline

11

to grasp even for an advanced student without a first-rate teacher to help, and the closest Chris had even come to a good teacher was Scranton's public librarian. She had tried hard; but she did not know the subject.

As a result, Chris stayed where he was. He would probably have done so even had he known positively that there was some danger; for in the valley, anything new was a change—even the fact, disastrous though it was, that Scranton was about to go as permanently out of his life and world as Betelgeuse. His own life thus far had held little but squirrel trapping; stealing eggs from neighbors as badly off as his own family; hunting scrap to sell to the mills; helping Bob nurse their father through repeated bouts of an illness which, but for the fact that there was no one in thirty-second-century America to diagnose it, would have been recognized as the ancient African scourge of *kwashiorkor* or malignant malnutrition; keeping the little girls out of the berry patch; fishing for fingerlings; and watching the rockets of the rich howl remotely through the highest reaches of the indifferent sky.

He had often thought of leaving, though he had no trade to practice and knew of no place in the world where his considerable but utterly untrained brute strength could be sold at any price. But there was loyalty and love in the motherless family, and it had often before sustained them when there had been nothing to eat but fried dough and green tomatoes, and no warmth against the Christmas snows but huddling with the little kids under a heap of the old rags that were their clothes; and in the end, Chris stuck by it as stubbornly and devotedly as Bob always had. In all the depopulated Earth there was no place to which he owed more loyalty, and no place which could offer him more in return—the worst possible substratum for dreams of escape, even for a temperament as natually sunny and sanguine as Chris's. In a world where a Ph.D. in economics could find no one to teach, nor use his knowledge of how the economy wagged to find any other niche in it—a world in which a thousand penny-ante jobs left him no time even to tend his wife's grave, yet all the same paid him less and less every year—what hope could his boys reasonably cherish for any better future? The answer, alas, was all too obvious; and for the little girls, the foreseeable future was even more grim.

The nomad cities offered no better way of escape. More often than not, Chris had read, star roving was simply another form of starvation, without even the company of a blue sky, a scrub forest or a patch of ground to grow turnips in. Otherwise, why did almost every city which had ever left the Earth fail to come back home? Pittsburgh had made its fortune on Mars, to be sure—but it was a poor sort of fortune that kept you sitting in a city all your life, with nothing to see beyond the city limits but an ochre desert, a desert with no air you could breath, a desert that would freeze you solid only a few minutes after the tiny sun went down. Sooner or later, too, his father said, Pittsburgh would have to leave the solar system as all the other cities had—not, this time, because it had exhausted the iron and the oxygen, but because there would be too few people left on the Earth to buy steel. There were already too few to justify Pittsburgh's coming back to the once-golden triangle of rivers it had abandoned thirty years ago; Pittsburgh had wealth, but was finding it increasingly hard to spend on the Earth, even for necessities. The nomad cities seemed, like everything else, to be a dead end.

Nevertheless Chris sat on the embankment and watched, for only a single, simple reason: Something was going on. If he envied the city its decision to leave the valley, he was unaware of it. He was there simply to see something happen, for a change.

A brief rustle of shrubbery behind him made him

13

turn. A dog's head peered across the roadbed at him from the foot of the mountainside, surrounded incongruously by the trumpets of tiger lilies; it looked a little as if it were being served up on a platter. Chris grinned.

"Hello, Kelly. Look out for bees."

The dog whuffed and came trotting to him, looking foolishly proud of itself—as it probably was, for Kelly was usually not very good at finding anything, even his own way home. Bob, whose dog Kelly officially was, said that Kelly was a combination of Kerry blue and collie—hence the name—but Chris had never seen a pure sample of either breed, and Kelly did not look anything like the pictures of either. He looked, in point of fact, like a shaggy mutt, which was fortunate for him, since that was what he was.

"What do you make of it, handsome? Think they'll ever get that thing off the ground?"

Kelly gave an imitation of a dog trying to think, registered pain, wagged his tail twice, woofed at a butterfly and sat down, panting. It had obviously always been his impression that he belonged to Chris, an impression Bob had wisely never tried to discourage. Explaining something that abstract to Kelly was (a) a long and complicated task, and (b) utterly hopeless anyhow. Kelly earned his own keep—he caught rabbits—which made up for the nuisance he was when he caught a porcupine; so nobody in the family but Chris much cared whom he thought he belonged to.

There was at last some activity around the parching city. Small groups of men, made so tiny by distance that they were almost invisible except for their bright yellow steelworkers' helmets, were patrolling the bare perimeter. There was probably a law about that, Chris reflected. Equally probably it would be the last Earth law Scranton would ever be *obliged* to observe—no matter how many of them the city fathers took into space of their own free will. No doubt the patrol was

14

looking for rubbernecks who might be standing too close for safety.

He imagined it so vividly that for a moment he had the illusion of hearing their voices. Then he realized with a start that it was not an illusion. A flash of yellow hard hats revealed another group of patrollers working their way through the shacks at the foot of the embankment and coming in his direction.

With the ingrained prudence of the lifelong poacher, he took at once to the bushes on the other side of the roadbed. Not only would he be invisible from there, but, of course, he could no longer see the patrol; however, he could still hear it.

". . . anybody in these shacks. Ask me, it's a waste of time."

"The boss says look, so we look, that's all. Myself, I think we'd make out better in Nixonville."

"Them tramps? They can smell work ten miles away. People on this side of town, they used to *look* for work. Not that there ever was any."

Chris cautiously parted the shrubbery and peered out. The gang was still out of sight, but there was another group coming toward him from the other direction, walking along the old roadbed. He let the bushes swing closed hastily, wishing that he had retreated farther up the mountainside. It was too late for that now, though. The new patrol was close enough to hear the brush rustle, and would probably see him too if he was in motion.

Down in the valley there was a sudden, slight hum, like bee-buzz, but infinitely gentler, and deeper in tone. Chris had never heard anything exactly like it before, but there could be no doubt in his mind about what it was: Scranton's spindizzies were being tuned. Was he going to have to hide right through the take-off, and miss seeing it? But surely the city wouldn't leave until its patrols were back on board!

The voices came closer, and beside him Kelly growled softly. The boy grasped the dog firmly by the scruff and shook him gently, not daring to speak. Kelly shut up, but all his muscles were tensed.

"Hey! Look what we got here!"

Chris froze as completely as a rabbit smelling fox; but another voice struck in at once.

"You guys get outa here. This here's my place. You got no business with me."

"Yeah? You didn't hear anything about getting out of the valley by noon today? There's a poster on your own front door that says so. Can't read, huh, Jack?"

"I don't do everything any piece of paper says. I live here, see? It's a lousy dump, but it's mine, and I'm staying, that's all. Now blow, will you?"

"Well, now, I don't know if that's all, Jack. It's the law that you're supposed to be vacated. *We* don't want your shack, but it's the law, see?"

"It's the law that I got a right to my own property, too."

A new voice chimed in from the embankment, not fifteen feet from where Chris and Kelly crouched. "Trouble down there, Barney?"

"Squatter. Won't move. Says he owns the place."

"That's a laugh. Get him to show you his deed."

"Ah, why bother with that? We ain't got the time. Let's impress him and get moving."

"*No you don't—*"

There was the meaty sound of a blow landing, and a grunt of surprise. "Hey, he wants to play rough! All right, mister—"

More impacts, and then the sound of something smashing—glass or crockery, Chris guessed, but it might have been furniture. Before Chris could do more than grab at him convulsively, Kelly burst into a volley of high, howling yelps, broke free, crashed out of the

16

bushes and went charging across the embankment toward the fracas.

"Look out! Hey—Where'd that mutt come from?"

"Out of the bushes there. Somebody's in there still. Red hair, I can see it. All right, Red, out in the open— on the double!"

Chris rose slowly, ready to run or fight at the drop of a hard hat. Kelly, on the far side of the embankment, gave up his idiot barking for a moment, his attention divided between the struggle in the shack and the group now surrounding Chris.

"Well, Red, you're a husky customer. I suppose you didn't hear about any vacate order, either."

"No, I didn't," Chris said defiantly. "I live in Lakebranch. I only came over to watch."

"Lakebranch?" the leader said, looking at another of his leathery-faced patrolmates.

"Hick town, way out back some place. Used to be a resort. Nothing out there now but poachers and scratchers."

"That's nice," the other man said, tipping back his yellow helmet and grinning. "Nobody'll miss you, I guess, Red. Come along."

"What do you mean, come along?" Chris said, his fists clenching. "I have to be home by five."

"Watch it—the kid's got some beef on him."

The other man, now clearly in charge, laughed scornfully. "You scared? He's a kid, isn't he? Come on, Red, I got no time to argue. You're here past noon, we got a legal right to impress you."

"I told you, I'm duo homo."

"You should have thought of that before you came here. Move along. You give us a hard time, we give you one, get it?"

Below, three men came out of the shack, holding hard to the gardener Chris had seen earlier. All looked considerably battered, but the sullen red-neck was secured all the same.

"We got this one—no thanks to you guys. Thought you was going to be right down. Big help you was!"

"Got another one, Barney. Let's go, Red."

The press-gang leader took Chris by the elbow. He was not unnecessarily violent about it, but the movement was sudden enough to settle matters in Kelly's slow brain. Kelly was unusually stupid, even for a dog, but he now knew which fight interested him most. With a snarl which made even Chris's hackles rise—he had never in his life before heard a dog make such a noise, let alone Kelly—the animal streaked back across the embankment and leaped for the big man's legs.

In the next thirty seconds of confusion Chris might easily have gotten away—there were a hundred paths through the undergrowth that he might have taken that these steel puddlers would have found it impossible to follow—but he couldn't abandon Kelly. And with an instinct a hundred thousand years old, the patrol fell on the animal enemy first, turning their backs on the boy without even stopping to think.

Chris was anything but a trained in-fighter, but he had instincts of his own. The man with Kelly's teeth in him was obviously busy enough. Chris lobbed a knob-kerrie fist at the man next to him. When the target looked stunned but failed to fall, Chris threw the other fist. It didn't land where Chris had meant it to land, exactly, but the man staggered away anyhow, which was good enough. Then Chris was in the middle of the melee and no longer had any chance even to try to call his shots.

After a while, he was on the broken granite of the old roadbed, and no longer cared about Scranton, Kelly or even himself. His head was ringing. Over him, considerable swearing was going on.

"—more trouble than he's worth. Give him a shoe in the head and let's get back!"

"No. No killing. We can impress 'em, but we can't bump 'em off. One of you guys see if you can slap Huggins awake."

"What are you—chicken all of a sudden?"

The press-gang leader was breathing hard, and as Chris's sight cleared, he saw that the big man was sitting on the ground wrapping a bloody leg in a length of torn shirt. Nevertheless he said evenly: "You want to kill a kid because he gave you a fight? That's the lousiest excuse for killing a man I ever heard, let alone a kid. You give me any more of that, I'll take a poke at you myself."

"Ah, shaddup, will you?" the other voice said surlily. "Anyhow we got the dog—"

"You loud-mouthed—*look out!*"

Two men grabbed Chris, one from each side, as he surged to his feet. He struggled fiercely, but all the fight left in him was in his soul, not any in his muscles.

"What a bunch of flap-jaws. No wonder you can't hold your own with a kid. Huggins, put your hat on. Red, don't you listen to that slob, he's been all mouth all his life. Your dog ran away, that's all."

The lie was kindly meant, no matter how clumsy it was, but it was useless. Chris could see Kelly, not far away. Kelly had done the best he could; he would never have another chance.

The youngster the press-gang dragged stumbling toward Scranton had a heart made of stone.

2

A LINE OF BOILING DUST

The city inside the perimeter of raw earth was wavery and unreal. It did not hum any more, but it gave a puzzling impression of being slightly in shadow, though the July sun was still blazing over it. Even in his grief and anger, Chris was curious enough to wonder at the effect, and finally he thought he saw what caused it: The heat waves climbing the air around the town seemed to be detouring it, as though the city itself were inside a dome. No, not a dome, but a bubble, only a part of which was underground; it met the earth precisely at the cleared perimeter.

The spindizzy field was up. It was invisible in itself, but it was no longer admitting the air of the Earth.

Scranton was ready.

Thanks to the scrapping, the patrol was far behind schedule; the leader drove them all through the scabrous, deserted suburbs without any mercy for his own torn leg. Chris grimly enjoyed watching him wince at every other step, but the man did not allow the wound to hold him up, nor did he let any of the lesser bruises and black eyes in the party serve as excuses for foot dragging.

There was no way to tell, by the normal human senses, when the party passed through the spindizzy screen. Midway across the perimeter, which was a good five hundred feet wide, the leader unshipped from his belt a device about as big as an avocado, turned it in his hands until it whined urgently, and then directed the group on ahead of him in single file, along a line which he traced in the dry red ground with the toe of his boot.

As his two guards left his side, Chris crouched instinctively. He was not afraid of them, and the leader apparently was going to stay behind. But the big man saw the slight motion.

"Red, I wouldn't if I were you," he said quietly. "If you try to run back this way after I turn off this gadget —or if you try to go around me—you'll go straight up in the air. Look back and see the dust rising. You're a lot heavier than a dust speck, and you'll go up a lot farther. Better relax. Take it from me."

Chris looked again at the dubious boundary line he had just crossed. Sure enough, there was a hair-thin ruling there, curving away to both sides as far as he could see, where the inert friable earth seemed to be turning over restlessly. It was as though he were standing inside a huge circle of boiling dust.

"That's right, that's what I meant. Now look here." The press-gang leader bent and picked up a stone just about as big as his fist—which was extraordinarily big —and shied it back the way they had come. As the rock started to cross the line above the seething dust, it leaped skyward with an audible screech, like a bullet ricocheting. In less than a second, Chris had lost sight of it.

"Fast, huh? And it'd throw you much farther, Red. In a few minutes, it'll be lifting a whole city. So don't go by how things look. Right where you stand, you're not even on the Earth any more."

Chris looked at the mountains for a moment, and then back at the line of boiling dust. Then he turned away and resumed marching toward Scranton.

And yet they were now on a street Chris had traveled a score of times before, carrying fifty cents for the Sunday paper's Help Wanted ads, or rolling a wheelbarrow not quite full of rusty scrap, or bringing back a flat package of low-grade ground horsemeat. The difference lay only in the fact that just beyond the familiar corner the city stopped, giving place to the new desert of the perimeter—and all in the overarching shadow which was not a shadow at all.

The patrol leader stopped and looked back. "We'll never make it from here," he said finally. "Take cover. Barney, watch that red-neck. I'll take the kid with me; he looks sensible."

Barney started to answer, but his reply was drowned out by a prolonged fifty-decibel honking which made the very walls howl back. The noise was horrifying; Chris had never before heard anything even a fraction so loud, and it seemed to go on forever. The press-gang boss herded him into a doorway.

"There's the alert. Duck, you guys. Stand still, Red. There's probably no danger—we just don't know. But something might just shake down and fall—so keep your head in."

The honking stopped; but in its place Chris could again hear the humming, now so pervasive that it made his teeth itch in their sockets. The shadow deepened, and out in the bare belt of earth the seething dust began to leap into the air in feathery plumes almost as tall as ferns.

Then the doorway lurched and went askew. Chris grabbed for the frame; and just in time, for a second later, the door jerked the other way; and then, back again. Gradually, the quakes became periodic, spacing themselves farther apart in time, and slowly weakening in violence.

After the first quake, however, Chris's alarm began to dwindle into amazement, for the movements of the ground were puny compared to what was going on before his eyes. The whole city seemed to be rocking heavily, like a ship in a storm. At one instant, the street ended in nothing but sky; at the next, Chris was staring at a wall of sheared earth, its rim looming clifflike, fifty feet or more above the new margin of the city; and then the blank sky was back again—

These huge pitching movements should have brought the whole city down in a roaring avalanche of steel and stone. Instead, only these vague twitchings and shudderings of the ground came through, and even those seemed to be fading away. Now the city was level again, amidst an immense cloud of dust, through which Chris could see the landscape begin to move solemnly past him. The city had stopped rocking, and was now turning slowly. There was no longer even the slightest sensation of movement; the illusion that it was the valley that was revolving around the city was irresistible and more than a little dizzying.

I can see where the spindizzy got its name, Chris thought. *Wonder if we go around like a top all the time we're in space? How'll we see where we're going, then?*

But now the high rim of the valley was sinking. In a breath, the distant roadbed of the railroad embankment was level with the end of the street; then the lip of the street was at the brow of the mountain; then with the treetops . . . and then there was nothing but blue sky, becoming rapidly darker.

The big press-gang leader released an explosive sigh. "By thunder," he said, "we got her up." He seemed a little dazed. "I guess I never really believed it till now."

"Not so sure I believe it yet," the man called Barney said. "But I don't see any cornices falling—we don't have to hang around here any longer. The boss'll have our necks for being even this late."

"Yeah, let's move. Red, use your head and don't give

23

us any more trouble, huh? You can see for yourself, there's no place to run to now."

There was no doubt about that. The sky at the end of the street, and overhead too, was now totally black; and even as Chris looked up, the stars became visible —at first only a few of the brightest, but the others came out steadily in their glorious hundreds. From their familiar fixity Chris could also deduce that the city was no longer rotating on its axis, which was vaguely reassuring, somehow. Even the humming had faded away again; if it was still present, it was now inaudible in the general noise of the city.

Oddly, the sunlight was still as intense as ever. From now on, "day" and "night" would be wholly arbitrary terms aboard the city; Scranton had emerged into the realm of Eternal Daylight-Saving Time.

The party walked two blocks and then stopped while the big man located a cab post and pulled the phone from it. Barney objected at once.

"It'll take a fleet of cabs to get us all to the Hall," he complained. "And we can't get enough guys into a hack to handle a prisoner, if he gets rough."

"The kid won't get rough. Go ahead and march your man over. I'm not going to walk another foot on this leg."

Barney hesitated, but obviously the big man's marked limp was an unanswerable argument. Finally he shrugged and herded the rest of his party around the corner. His boss grinned at Chris; but the boy looked away.

The cab came floating down out of the sky at the intersection and maneuvered itself to rest at the curb next to them with a finicky precision. There was, of course, nobody in it; like everything else in the world requiring an I.Q. of less than 150, it was computer-controlled. The world-wide dominance of such machines, Chris's father had often said, had been one of the chief contributors to the present and apparently permanent depression: the coming of semi-intelligent machines into business and technology had created a second Industrial Revolution, in which only the most highly creative human beings, and those most gifted at administration, found themselves with any skills to sell which were worth the world's money to buy.

Chris studied the cab with the liveliest interest, for though he had often seen them before from a distance, he had of course never ridden in one. But there was very little to see. The cab was an egg-shaped bubble of light metals and plastics, painted with large red-and-white checkers, with a row of windows running all around it. Inside, there were two seats for four people, a speaker grille, and that was all; no controls, and no instruments. There was not even any visible place for the passenger to deposit his fare.

The big press-gang leader gestured Chris into the front seat, and himself climbed into the back. The doors slid shut simultaneously from the ceiling and floor, rather like a mouth closing, and the cab lifted gently until it hovered about six feet above street level.

"Destination?" the Tin Cabby said cheerily, making Chris jump.

"City Hall."

"Social Security number?"

"One five six one one dash zero nine seven five dash zero six nine eight two one seven."

"Thank you."

"Shaddup."

"You're welcome, sir."

The cab lifted vertically, and the gang captain settled back into his seat. He seemed content for the moment to allow Chris to sight-see out the windows at the passing stubby towers of the flying city; he looked relaxed and a little indulgent, but a little wary, too. Finally he said:

"I need to dutch-uncle you a little, Red. I didn't call

25

a cab because of the leg—I've walked farther on worse. Feel up to listening?"

Chris felt himself freezing. Distracted though he was by all this enormous budget of new experience and the vast reaches of the unknown which stretched before him, the press-gang leader's remark reminded him instantly of Kelly, and as instantly made him ashamed that he had forgotten. In the same rush of anger he remembered that he had been kidnapped, and that now there was no one left to take care of his father and the little kids but Bob. That had been hard enough to do when there had been two of them. It was bad enough that he would never see Annie and Kate and Bob and his father again, but far worse that they should be deprived of his hands and his back and his love; and worst of all, they would never know what had happened.

The little girls would only think that he and Kelly had run away, and wonder why, and mourn a little until they forgot about it. But Bob and his father might well think that he'd deserted them . . . most likely of all, that he had gone off with Scranton on his own hook, leaving them all to scrounge for themselves.

There was a well-known ugly term for that among the peasantry of the Earth, expressing all the contempt it felt for any man who abandoned his land, no matter how unrewarding it was, to tread the alien streets and star lanes of a nomad city: it was called, "going Okie."

Chris had gone Okie. He had not done it of his own free will, but his father and Bob and the little girls would never know that. For that matter, it would never have happened had it not been for his own useless curiosity; and neither would the death of poor Kelly, who, Chris now remembered too, had been Bob's dog.

The big man in the hard hat saw his expression close down, and made an impatient gesture. "Listen, Red, I know what you're thinking. What good would it do now if I said I was sorry? What's done is done; you're on board, and you're going to stay on board. We didn't put the snatch on you either. If you didn't know about the impressment laws, you've got your own ignorance to blame."

"You killed my brother's dog."

"No, I didn't. I've got a bad rip or two under that rag to prove I had reasons to kill him; but I wasn't the guy who did it, and I wouldn't have done it, either. But that's done too, and can't be undone. Right now I'm trying to help you, and I've got about three minutes left to do it in, so if you don't shut up and listen it'll be too late. You *need* help, Red; can't you understand that?"

"Why do you bother?" Chris said bitterly.

"Because you're a bright kid and a fighter, and I like that. But that's not going to be enough aboard an Okie city, believe me. You're in a situation now that's totally new to you, and if you've got any skills you can make a career on here, I'll be darned surprised, I can tell you that. And Scranton isn't going to start educating you this far along in your life. Are you smart enough to take some advice, or aren't you? If you aren't, there's no sense in my bothering. You've got about a minute left to think it over."

What the big man said made a bitter dose to have to swallow, but it did seem to make sense. And it did seem likely, too, that the man's intentions were good—otherwise, why would he be taking the trouble? Nevertheless Chris's emotions were in too much of a turmoil for him to trust himself to speak; instead, he merely nodded mutely.

"Good for you. First of all, I'm taking you to see the boss—not the mayor, he doesn't count for much, but Frank Lutz, the city manager. One of the things he'll ask you is what you do, or what you know about. Between now and when we get there, you ought to be thinking up an answer. I don't care what you tell him,

27

but tell him *something*. And it had better be the thing you know the most about, because he'll ask you questions."

"I don't know anything—except gardening, and hunting," Chris said grimly.

"No, no, that's not what I mean! Don't you have any book subjects? Something that might be useful in space? If you don't, he'll put you to work pitching slag—and you won't have much of a lifetime as an Okie."

The cab slowed, and then began to settle.

"And if he doesn't seem interested in what you tell him, *don't* try to satisfy him by switching to something else. No true specialist really knows more than one subject, especially at your age. Stick to the one you picked and try to make it sound useful. Understand?"

"Yes, but—"

"No time left for 'buts.' One other thing: If you ever get into a jam on board this burg, you'll need to know somebody to turn to, and it'd better not be Frank Lutz. My name is Frad Haskins—not Fred but Frad, F-R-A-D."

The cab hovered for a moment, and then its hull grated against cobblestones and the doors slid open. Chris was thinking so hard and in so many directions that for a long moment he did not understand what the press-gang chief was trying to convey by introducing himself. Then the realization hit home, and Chris was struggling unsuccessfully to blurt out his thanks and to give his own name at the same time.

"Destination, gentlemen," the Tin Cabby said primly. "Shaddup. Come along, Red."

Frank Lutz, the city manager of Scranton-in-flight, reminded Chris instantly of a skunk—but by this Chris meant not at all what a city boy would have meant by a skunk. Lutz was small, sleek, handsome, and plump, and even sitting behind his desk, he gave an appearance of slight clumsiness. As he listened to Haskins' account

28

of the two impressments, even his expression had something of the nearsighted amiability of the wood pussy; but as Haskins finished, the city manager looked up suddenly—and Chris knew, if he had ever been in any doubt about it before, that this animal was also dangerous . . . and never more so than when it seemed to be turning its back.

"That impressment law was a nuisance. But I suppose we'll have to make a show of maintaining our pickups until we get to some part of space where the police aren't so thick."

"We've got no drug for them, that's for sure," Haskins agreed obscurely.

"That's not a public subject," Lutz said, with such deadly coldness that Chris was instantly convinced that the slip, whatever its meaning, had been intended by Haskins for his own ears. The big man was a lot more devious than his size or his bluffness suggested. That much was becoming clearer every minute. "As for these samples, I don't suppose they can do anything. They never can."

The deceptively mild hazel eyes, watery and inoffensive, swung suddenly to bear on the red-neck. "What's your name?"

"Who wants to know? That's what I want to know. You got no right—"

"Don't buck me, bum, I haven't got the time. So you've got no name. Have you a trade?"

"I'm no bum, 'm a puddler," the red-neck said indignantly. "A *steel* puddler."

"Same thing. Anything else?"

"I been a puddler twenty years. 'M a Master Puddler, fair an' square. I got seniority, see? I don' need to be anything else, see? I got a trade. Nobody knows it like I do."

"Been working lately?" the city manager said quietly.

29

"No. But I got seniority. And a card. 'M no bum, 'm a craftsman, see?"

"If you were a Genius Puddler I couldn't use you, buddy . . . not even if, as and when we ever see any steel again. This is a Bessemer-process town, and it was one even back when you were an apprentice. You didn't notice? Tough. Barney, Huggins, this one's for the slag heaps."

This order was not executed without a good deal of renewed shouting and struggling, during which Lutz looked back down at his papers, as obviously harmless a critter as a skunk which had just happened upon a bird's egg and was wondering if it might bite, his small hands moving tentatively. When the noise was over, he said:

"I hope your luck was better, Frad. How about it, sonny? Have you got a trade?"

"Yes," Chris said instantly. "Astronomy."

"What? At your age?" The city manager stared at Haskins. "What's this, Frad—another one of your mercy projects? Your judgment gets worse every day."

"It's all news to me, boss," Haskins said with complete and obvious honesty. "I thought he was just a scratcher. He never said anything else to me."

The city manager drummed delicately on the top of his desk. Chris held his breath. His claim was ridiculous and he knew it, but he had been able to think of nothing else to answer which would have had a prayer of interesting the boss of a nomad city. Insofar as he had been able to stay awake past dusk, Chris had read a little of everything, and of his reading he had retained best the facts and theories of history; but Haskins had cautioned him to espouse something which might be useful aboard an Okie city, and plainly it didn't qualify. The fragments of economics he had picked up from his father might possibly have been more useful had there been more of them, and those better integrated into *recent* history, but his father had never been well enough to do that job since Chris had reached the age of curiosity. He was left with nothing but his smattering of astronomy, derived from books, most of which had been published before he was born, and from many nights spent lying on his back in the fields, breathing clover and counting meteors.

But he had no hope that it would work. A nomad city would need astronomy for navigation, primarily, a subject about which he knew nothing—indeed he lacked even the rudimentary trigonometry necessary to approach it. His knowledge of the parent subject, astronomy, was purely descriptive, and would become obsolete the minute Scranton was far enough away from the Sun to make the constellations hard to recognize—which in fact had probably happened already.

Nevertheless, Frank Lutz seemed to be a little bit baffled, for the first time. He said slowly:

"A Lakebranch kid who claims he's an astronomer! Well, at least it's new. Frad, you've let the kid sell you a hobby. If he ever got through grammar school I'll eat your tin hat, paint and all."

"Boss, I swear I never heard a word of all this until now."

"Hmm. All right, sonny. Name the planets, going outward from the Sun."

That was easy, but the next ones would surely be harder. "Mercury, Venus, Earth, Mars, Jupiter, Saturn, Uranus, Neptune, Pluto, Proserpina."

"You left out a few didn't you?"

"I left out about five thousand," Chris said, as steadily as he could manage. "You said planets—not asteroids or satellites."

"All right, what's the biggest satellite? And the biggest asteroid?"

"Titan, and Ceres."

"What's the nearest fixed star?"

31

"The Sun."

The city manager grinned, but he did not seem to be much amused. "Oho. Well, it won't be, not much longer. How many months in a light-year?"

"Twelve, just like any other year. A light-year isn't a measure of time, it's a measure of distance—the distance light travels in a year. Months don't have anything to do with it. You might as well ask how many weeks there are in an inch."

"There are fifty-two weeks to the inch—or it'll seem like that, once you're as old as I am." Lutz drummed on the desk again. "Where'd you get all this stuff? You won't pretend you had any schooling in Lakebranch, I hope?"

"My father taught almost all his life at the University, till it was shut down," Chris said. "He was the best there was. I got most of it from him. The rest I read about, or got from observation, and paper and pencil."

Here Chris was on firm ground, provided only that he be allowed one lie: the substitution of astronomy for economics. The next question did not bother him in the least, for it was thoroughly expectable:

"What's your name?"

"Crispin deFord," he said reluctantly.

There was a surprised guffaw from the remainder of the audience, but Chris did his best to ignore it. His ridiculous name had been a burden to him through so many childhood fights with the neighbors that he was now able to carry it with patience, though still not very gladly. He was surprised, however, to see Haskins raising his bushy bleached eyebrows at him with every evidence of renewed interest. What that meant, Chris had no idea; the part of his brain that did his guessing was almost worn out already.

"Check that, somebody," the city manager said. "We've got a couple of people left over from the S. U.

faculty, at least. By Hoffa, Boyle Warner was a Scranton prof, wasn't he? Get him up here, and let's close this thing out."

"What's the matter, boss?" Haskins said, with a broad grin. "Running out of trick questions?"

The city manager smiled back, but again the smile was more than a little frosty. "You could call it that," he said, with surprising frankness. "But we'll see if the kid can fool Warner."

"The ole bassar must be good for something," somebody behind Chris mumbled. The voice was quiet, but the city manager heard it; his chin jerked up, and his fist struck a sudden, terrible blow on the top of his desk.

"He's good for getting us where we're going, and don't you forget it! Steel is one thing, but stars are another—we may never see another lie or another ingot without Boyle. Next to him we're *all* puddlers, just like that red-neck. And that may go for the kid here, too."

"Ah, boss, don't lay it on. What can *he* know?"

"That's what I'm trying to find out," Lutz said, in a white fury. "What do you know about it? Anybody here know what a geodesic is?"

Nobody answered.

"Red, do you know?"

Chris swallowed. He knew the answer, but he found it impossible to understand why the city manager considered it worth all this noise.

"Yes, sir. It's the shortest distance between two points."

"Is that all?" somebody said incredulously.

"It's all there is between us and starvation," Lutz said. "Frad, take the kid below and see what Boyle says about him; on second thought, I don't want to pull Boyle out of the observatory, he must be up to his eyebrows in course-corrections. Get to Boyle as soon as he's got some free time. Find out if there ever was any Professor deFord at S. U.; and then get Boyle to ask the kid some hard questions. *Real* hard. If he makes it, he can be an apprentice. If he doesn't, there are always the slag heaps; this has taken too long already."

3

"LIKE A BARREL OF SCRAP"

Even a city which has sloughed off its slums to go space flying has hidey holes, and Chris had lost no time in finding one of his own. He had located it with the simple instinct of a hunted animal going to ground.

Not that anybody was hunting for him—not yet. But something told him that it would be only a matter of time. Dr. Boyle Warner, the city's astronomer, had been more than kind to him, but he had asked hard questions all the same; and these had revealed quickly enough that Chris's knowledge of astronomy, while extraordinary in a youngster with no formal education worth mentioning, was too meager to be of any help to Dr. Warner or of any use to the city.

Dr. Warner signed him on as an apprentice anyhow, and so reported to the city manager's office, but not without carefully veiled misgivings, and an open warning:

"I can think of very little for you to do around the observatory that would be useful, Crispin, I'm sorry to say. If I so much as set you to work sweeping the place, one of Frank Lutz's henchmen would find out about it sooner or later; and Frank would point out quite legitimately that I don't need so big a fellow as you for so light a task as that. While you're with me, you'll have to appear to be studying all the time."

"I will be studying," Chris said. "That's just what I'd like."

"I appreciate that," Dr. Warner said sadly. "And I sympathize. But Crispin, it can't last forever. Neither I nor anyone else in Scranton can give you in two years the ten years of study that you've missed, let alone any part of what it took me thirty more years to absorb. I'll do my best, but that best can only be a pretense—and sooner or later they'll catch us at it."

After that, Chris already knew, would come the slag heaps—hence the hidey hole. He wondered if they would send Dr. Warner to the slag heaps too. It didn't seem very likely, for the frail, pot-bellied little astrophysicist could hardly last long at the wrong end of a shovel, and besides he was the only navigator the city had. Chris mentioned this guardedly to Frad Haskins.

"Don't you believe it," Frad said grimly. "The fact is that we've got no navigator at all. Expecting an astronomer to navigate is about like asking a chicken to fry an egg. Doc Warner ought to be a navigator's assistant himself, not a navigator-in-chief, and Frank Lutz knows it. If we ever run across another city with a spare *real* navigator to trade, Frank could send Boyle Warner to the slag heaps without blinking an eye. I don't say that he would, but he might."

It could hardly be argued that Haskins knew his boss, and after only one look of his own at Lutz, Chris was more than ready to agree. Officially, Chris continued to occupy the single tiny room at the university dormitory to which he had been assigned as Dr. Warner's apprentice, but he kept nothing there but the books that Dr. Warner lent him, the mathematical instruments from the same source, and the papers and charts that he was supposed to be working on; plus about a quarter of the rough clothing and the even rougher food which the city had issued him as soon as he had been given an official status. The other three-quarters of both went into the hole, for Chris had no intention of letting himself be caught at an official address when the henchmen of Frank Lutz finally came looking for him.

He studied as hard in the hole as he did in the dormitory and at the observatory, all the same. He was firmly determined that Dr. Warner should not suffer for his dangerous kindness if there was anything that Chris could possibly do to avoid it. Frad Haskins, though his visits were rare—he had no real business at the university—detected this almost at once; but he said only:

"I knew you were a fighter."

For almost a year Chris was quite certain that he was making progress. Thanks to his father, for example, he found it relatively easy to understand the economy of the city—probably better than most of its citizens did, and almost certainly better than either Frad Haskins or Dr. Warner. Once aloft, Scranton had adopted the standard economy of all tribes of highly isolated nomad herdsmen, to whom the only real form of wealth is grass: a commune, within which everyone helped himself to what he needed, subject only to the rules which established the status of his job in the community. If Frad Haskins needed to ride in a cab, for instance, he boarded it, and gave the Tin Cabby his social security number—but if, at the end of the fiscal year, his account showed more cab charges than was reasonable for his job, he would hear about it. And if he or anyone else took to hoarding physical goods—no matter whether they were loaves of bread or lock washers, they could not by definition be in anything but short supply on board an Okie city—he would do more than hear about it: The penalties for hoarding of any kind were immediate and drastic.

There was money aboard the city, but no ordinary citizen ever saw it or needed it. It was there to be used exclusively for foreign trade—that is, to bargain for graz-

ing rights, or other privileges and supplies which the
city did not and could not carry within the little universe bounded by its spindizzy field. The ancient herdsmen had accumulated gold and jewels for the same
reason. Aboard Scranton, the equivalent metal was
germanium, but there was actually very little of it in
the city's vaults; since germanium had been the universal metal base for money throughout this part of the
galaxy ever since space flight had become practical, most
of the city's currency was paper—the same "Oc dollar"
everyone used in trading with the colonies.

All this was new to Chris in the specific situation in
which he now found himself, but it was far from new
to him in principle. As yet, however, he was too lowly
an object in Scranton to be able to make use of his understanding; and remembering the penury into which
his father had been driven, back on Earth, he was far
from sure that he would ever have a use for it.

As the year passed, so also did the stars. The city
manager, according to Haskins, had decided not to
cruise anywhere inside "the local group"—an arbitrary
sphere fifty light-years in diameter, with Sol at its cen-
ter. The planetary systems of the local group had been
heavily settled during the great colonial Exodus of 2200–
2400, mostly by people from Earth's fallen Western culture who were fleeing the then world-wide Bureaucratic State. It was Lutz's guess—quickly confirmed by
challenges received by Scranton's radio station—that the
density of older Okie cities would be too high to let a
newcomer into competition.

During this passage, Chris busied himself with trying
to identify the stars involved by their spectra. This was
the only possible way to do it under the circumstances,
for of course their positions among the constellations
changed rapidly as the city overtook them. So did the
constellations themselves, although far more slowly.

It was hard work, and Chris was often far from sure

his identifications were correct. All the same, it was impressive to know that those moving points of light all around him were the almost legendary stars of colonial times, and even more impressive to find that he had one of those storied suns in the small telescope. Their very names echoed with past adventure: Alpha Centauri, Wolf 359, RD–4°4048′, Altair, 61 Cygni, Sirius, Kruger 60, Procyon, 40 Eridani. Only a very few of these, of course, lay anywhere near the city's direct line of flight—indeed, many of them were scattered "astern" (that is, under the keel of the city), in the imaginary hemisphere on the other side of his home Sun. But most of them were at least visible from here, and the rest could be photographed. The city, whatever Chris thought of it as a home, had to be given credit for being a first-class observatory platform.

How he saw the stars was another matter, and one that was a complete mystery to him. He knew that Scranton was now traveling at a velocity many times that of light, and it seemed to him that under these circumstances there should have been no stars at all still visible in the city's wake, and those to the side and even straight ahead should be suffering considerable distortion. Yet in fact he could see no essential change in the aspect of the skies. To understand how this could be so would require at least some notion of how the spindizzies worked, and on this theory Dr. Warner's explanations were even more unclear than usual . . . so much so that Chris suspected him of not understanding it any too well himself.

Lacking the theory, Chris's only clue was that the stars from Scranton-in-flight looked to him much as they always had from a field in the Pennsylvania backwoods, where the surrounding Appalachians had screened him from the sky glare of Scranton-on-the-ground. From this he deducted that the spindizzy screen, though itself invisible, cut down the apparent brightness of the stars by about three magnitudes, as had the atmosphere of the Earth in the region where Chris had lived. Again he didn't know the reason why, but he could see that the effect had some advantages. For instance, it blanked out many of the fainter stars completely to the naked eye, thus greatly reducing the confusing multitudes of stars which would otherwise have been visible in space. Was that really an unavoidable effect of the spindizzy field— or was it instead something imposed deliberately, as an aid to navigation?

"I'm going to ask Lutz that question myself," Dr. Warner said, when Chris proposed it. "It's no help to me; in fact, it takes all the fun out of being an astronomer in free space. And there's no time like the present. Come along, Crispin—I can't very well leave you in charge, and the only other logical place for Lutz to see an apprentice of mine is with me."

It seemed to Chris that nobody aboard Scranton ever said anything officially to him but "Come along," but he went. He did not relish the prospect of seeing the city manager again, but it was probably true that he would be safer under the astronomer's wing than he would be anyplace else; in fact, he was both surprised by, and a little admiring of, Dr. Warner's boldness.

But if Boyle Warner ever asked the question, Chris never heard the answer.

Frank Lutz did not believe in making people who came to see him on official business wait in ante-chambers. It wasted his time as well as theirs, and he at least had none to waste—and they had better not have. Nor were there many details of his administration that he thought he needed to keep secret, not now that those who might oppose him no longer had any place to run to. To remind his people who was boss, he occasionally kept the mayor waiting out of earshot, but everyone else came and went quite freely when he held court.

Dr. Warner and Chris sat in the rearmost benches—

for Lutz's "court" was actually held in what once had been a courtroom—and waited patiently to work their way forward to the foot of the city manager's desk. In the process, the astronomer fell into a light doze; Frank Lutz's other business was nothing to him, and in addition his hearing was no better than usual for a man his age. Both Chris's curiosity and his senses, on the other hand, shared the acuity of his youth, and the latter had been sharpened by almost a lifetime of listening and watching for the rustle of small animals in the brush; and the feeling of personal danger with which Frank Lutz had filled him on their first encounter was back again, putting a razor edge upon hearing and curiosity alike.

"We're in no position to temporize," the city manager was saying. "This outfit is big—the biggest there is—and it's offering us a fair deal. The next time we meet it, it may not be so polite, especially if we give it any sass this time around. I'm going to talk turkey with them."

"But what do they want?" someone said. Chris craned his neck, but he did not know the man who had spoken. Most of Lutz's advisers were nonentities, in any event— except for those like Huggins, who were outright thugs.

"They want us to veer off. They've analyzed our course and say we're headed for a region of space that they'd had staked out long before we showed up. Now this, let me point out, is actually all to the good. They have a preliminary survey of the area, and we don't— everything ahead of *us* is all alike, until we've had some experience of it. Furthermore, one of the things they offer in payment is a new course which they say will take us into an iron-bearing star cluster, very recently settled, where there's likely to be plenty of work for us."

"So *they* say."

"And I believe them," Lutz said sharply. "Everything they've said to me, they've also said on the open air, by Dirac transmitter. The cops have heard every word, not only locally, but wherever in the whole universe that there's a Dirac transceiver. Big as they are, they're not going to attempt to phony an open contract. The only question in my mind is, what ought to be the price?"

He looked down at the top of his desk. Nobody seemed to have any suggestions. Finally he looked up again and smiled coldly.

"I've thought of several, but the one I like best is this: They can help us run up our supplies. We haven't got the food to reach the cluster that they've designated— I'd hoped we'd make a planetfall long before we had to go that far—but that's something that they can't know, and that I'm not going to tell them."

"They'll know when you ask for the food, Frank—"

"I'm not such an idiot. Do you think any Okie city would ever sell food at *any* price? You might as well try to buy oxygen, or money. *I'm* going to ask them to throw in some minor piece of machinery or other, it doesn't matter what, and two or three technicians to man and service it; and as an evidence of good faith, I'll offer back for these oh-so-valuable technicians a big batch of our people—people that are of no use to us. There won't be so many of them that a town *that* size would have any difficulty in absorbing them—but to us, they'll represent just the number of extra mouths to feed that would prevent us from reaching the iron-bearing cluster that Amalfi's offered to guide us to. Food will never be mentioned. It'll be just a standard swap of personnel, under the usual Okie 'rule of discretion.'"

There was a long minute of respectful silence. Even Chris was forced to admire the ingenuity of the scheme, insofar as he understood it. Frank Lutz smiled again and added:

"And this way, we get rid of every single one of those useless bums and red-necks we had to take aboard under the impressment laws. The cops will never know it;

and neither will Amalfi; he has to carry enough food and, ah, medicines to maintain a crew of well over a million. He'll swallow another three hundred yokels without as much effort as you'd swallow an aspirin, and probably think it a fair trade for two technies and a machine that are useless to him. The most beautiful part of it all is, it might even *be* a fair trade—which brings me to my next point—"

But Chris did not stay to hear the next point. After a last, quick, regretful glance at the drowsing astronomer who had befriended him, he stole out of the court as silently as any poacher, and went to ground.

The hole was structurally an accident. Located in a warehouse at the edge of the city nearest the university, it was in the midst of an immense stack of heavy crates which evidently had shifted during the first few moments of take-off, thus forming a huge and unpredictable three-dimensional maze which no map of the city would ever show. By worrying a hole in the side of one crate with a pocketknife, Chris had found that it contained mining machinery (and, evidently, so did all the others, since they all bore the same stenciled code number). The chances were good, he thought, that the crates would not be unstacked until Scranton made its first planetfall; the city in flight would have nothing to dig into.

Nor did Chris have any reason to leave the hole, at least for now. The warehouse itself had a toilet he could visit, and seemed to be unfrequented; and of course it didn't need a watchman—Who would bother to steal heavy machinery, and where would they run with it? If he was careful not to set any fires with his candles—for the hole, although fairly well ventilated through the labyrinth, was always pitch dark—he would probably be safe until his food ran out. After that, he would have to take his chances . . . but he had been a poacher before.

But nothing in his plans had allowed for a visitor.

He heard the sounds of the approach from some distance and blew out his candle at once. Maybe it was only a casual prowler; maybe even only a strayed child —maybe, at the worst, another refugee from Lutz's flesh-trading deal, looking for a hole. There were plenty of holes amid the piled-up crates, and the way to this one was so complex that the two of them could live in the heap for weeks without encountering each other.

But his heart sank as he realized how quietly the footsteps were approaching. The newcomer was negotiating the maze with scarcely a false turn, let alone a noisy blunder.

Someone knew where he was—or at least knew where his hole was.

The footsteps became louder, slowed, and stopped. Now he could distinctly hear someone breathing.

Then the beam of a hand torch caught him full in the face.

"Hello, Chris. Make a light, huh?"

The voice was that of Frad Haskins. Anger and relief flooded through Chris at the same time. The big man had been his first friend, and almost his name-brother—for after all, Fradley O. Haskins is not much more ridiculous a name than Crispin deFord—but that blow of light in the face had been like a betrayal.

"I've only got candles. If you'd set the flashlight on end, it'd be just as good—maybe better."

"Okay." Haskins sat down on the floor, placing the torch on the small crate Chris used for a table, so that it made a round spot of light on the boards overhead. "Now tell me something. Just what do you think you're doing?"

"Hiding," Chris said, a little sullenly.

"I can see that. I knew what this place was from the day I saw you toting books into it. I have to keep in practice on this press-gang dodge; I'll need it some day on some other planet. But in your case, what's the sense? Don't you *want* to be transferred to a bigger city?"

"No, I don't. Oh, I can't say that Scranton's been like home to me. I hate it. I wish I could really go home. But Frad, at least I'm getting to know the place. I already knew part of it, back while it was on the ground. I don't want to be kidnapped twice, and go through it all again —aboard some city where I don't know even as much about the streets as I knew about Scranton—and maybe find out that I hate it even worse. And I don't like being swapped, like—like a barrel of scrap."

"Well, maybe I can't blame you for that—though it's standard Okie procedure, not anything that Lutz thought up in his own head. Do you know where the 'rule of discretion' came from?"

"No."

"From the trading of players between baseball teams. It's that old—more than a thousand years. The contract law that sanctions it is supposed to be a whale of a lot older, even."

"All right," Chris said. "It could even be Roman, I suppose. But Frad, I'm not a barrel of scrap and I still don't want to be swapped."

"Now that part of it," the big man said patiently, "is just plain silly. You've got no future in Scranton, and you ought to know it by now. On a really big town you could probably find something to do—and the least you'll get is some schooling. All our schools are closed, for good and forever. And another thing: We've only been aloft a year, and it's a cinch we've got some hard times ahead of us. An older town would be a darn sight safer—not absolutely safe, no Okie ever is; but safer."

"Are you going, too?"

Haskins laughed. "Not a chance. Amalfi must have

45

ten thousand of the likes of me. Besides, Lutz needs me. He doesn't know it, but he does."

"Well . . . then . . . I'd rather stay with you."

Haskins smote one fist into the other palm in exasperation. "Look, Red . . . Cripes, what do you say to this kid? Thanks, Chris; I—I'll remember that. But if I'm lucky, I'll have a boy of my own some day. This isn't the day. If you don't face facts right now, you aren't going to get a second chance. Listen, I'm the only guy who knows where you are, yet, but how long can that last? Do you know what Frank will do when he roots you out of a hole full of cached food? *Think,* please, will you?"

Chris's stomach felt as though he had just been thrown out of a window.

"I guess I never thought of that."

"You need practice. I don't blame you for that. But I'll tell you what Frank will do: *He'll have you shot.* And nobody else in town'll even raise an eyebrow. In the Okie lawbook, hoarding food comes under the head of endangering the survival of the city. Any such crime is a capital crime—and not only in Scranton, either."

There was a long silence. At last, Chris said quietly: "All right. Maybe it is better this way. I'll go."

"That's using your head," Haskins said gruffly. "Come on, then. We'll tell Frank you were sick. You *look* sick, right enough. But we'll have to hustle—the gigs leave in two hours."

"Can I take my books?"

"They're not yours, they're Boyle Warner's," Fred said impatiently. "I'll get 'em back to him later. Pick up the torch and let's go—you'll find plenty of books where you're going." He stopped suddenly and glared at Chris through the dim light. "Not that you care where you're going! You haven't even asked the name of the town."

This was true; he had not asked, and now that he came to think about it, he didn't care. But his curiosity came forward even through the gloom of the maze, and even through his despair. He said, "So I haven't. What is it?"

"New York."

4

SCHOOLROOM IN THE SKY

The sight from the gig was marvelous beyond all imagination: an island of towers, as tall as mountains, floating in a surfaceless, bottomless sea of stars. The gig was rocket-powered, so that Chris was also seeing the stars from space in all their jeweled majesty for the first time in his life; but the silent pride of the great human city, aloof in its spindizzy bubble—which was faintly visible from the outside—completely took precedence. Behind the gig, Scranton looked in comparison like a scuttleful of old stove bolts.

The immigrants were met at the perimeter by a broad-shouldered, crew-cut man of about forty, in a uniform which made all of Chris's hackles rise; cops were natural enemies, here as everywhere. But the perimeter sergeant, who gave his name as Anderson, did no more than herd them all into separate cubicles for interviews.

There was nobody in Chris's cubicle but Chris himself. He was seated before a small ledge or banquette, facing a speaker grille which was set into the wall. From this there issued the questions, and into this he spoke his answers. Most of the questions were simple matters of vital statistics—his name, his age, point of origin, date of boarding Scranton and so on—but he rather enjoyed answering them; the fact was that never before in his life had anyone been interested enough in him to ask them. In fact he himself did not know the answers to some of them.

It was also interesting to speculate on the identity of the questioner. It was a machine, Chris was almost sure, and one speaking not from any vocabulary of prerecorded words sounded by a human voice, but instead from some store of basic speech sounds which it combined and recombined as it went along. The result was perfectly understandable and nonmechanical, carrying many of the stigmata of real human speech—for example, the sentences emerged in natural speech rhythms, and with enough inflection so that key words and even punctuation could be distinguished—yet all the same he would never have mistaken it for a human voice. Whatever the difference was, he thought of it as though the device were speaking all in capital letters.

Even in an age long dominated by computers, to the exclusion, in many cases, of human beings, Chris had never heard of a machine with intelligence enough to be able to construct its speech in this fashion, let alone one intelligent enough to be given the wide discretionary latitude implied by the conduct of this interview. He had never before heard of a machine which referred to itself as "we," either.

"How much schooling had you had before you were impressed, Mr. deFord?"

"Almost none."

"Did you receive any schooling aboard Scranton?"

"A little. Actually it was only just tutoring—the kind of thing I used to get from my father, when he felt up to it."

"It is rather late to start, but we can arrange schooling for you if you wish—"

"Boy, do I!"

"That is the question. An accelerated secondary education is physically very trying. It is possible that you would have no need of it here, depending

49

UPON YOUR GOALS. DO YOU WISH TO BE A PASSENGER, OR
A CITIZEN?"

On the surface, this was a perfectly easy question.
What Chris most wanted to do was to go home and back
to being a citizen of nothing more complicated than the
Commonwealth of Pennsylvania, Western Common Market, Terran Confederation. He had had many bad nights
spent wondering how his family was doing without him,
and what they had thought of his disappearance, and he
was sure that he would have many more. Yet by the
same token, by now they had doubtless made whatever
adjustment was possible for them to the fact of his being
gone; and an even more brutal fact was that he was now
sitting on a metropolis of well over a million people
which was floating in empty space a good twenty light-
years away from Sol, bound for some destination he
could not even guess. This monstrous and wonderful
construct was not going to turn itself into his personal
Tin Cabby simply because he said he wanted to go
home, or for any other reason.

So if Chris was stuck with the city, he reasoned, he
might as well be a citizen. There was no point in being
a passenger when we had no idea where he was going,
or whether it would be worth the fare when he got
there. Being a citizen, on the other hand, sounded as
though it conferred some privileges; it would be worth
while knowing what they were. It would also be worth
knowing whether or not the two terms the machine had
used carried some special technical meaning of which
he ought to be wary.

"Who'm I talking to?"

"THE CITY FATHERS."

This reply nearly threw him completely off course;
he tabled the baker's dozen of questions it raised only
by a firm exercise of will. What was important about
it right now was that it told him that he was talking
to a responsible person—whatever the meaning of "Per-

son" might be when one is dealing with a machine with a collective personality.

"Am I entitled to ask questions too?"

"YES, WITHIN LIMITS IT WOULD TAKE TOO LONG TO DEFINE FOR THE PURPOSE OF THIS INTERVIEW. IF YOU ASK US QUESTIONS, WE WILL AT PRESENT EITHER ANSWER OR NOT ANSWER."

Chris thought hard. The City Fathers, despite their mention of time limitations, waited him out without any evidence of impatience. Finally he said:

"What's the most important single difference between a passenger and a citizen."

"A CITIZEN LIVES AN INDEFINITELY PROLONGED LIFE."

Nothing they could have said could have been farther from any answer that Chris might have expected. It was so remote from anything he had ever thought or read about that it was almost meaningless to him. Finally he managed to ask cautiously: "How long is indefinitely?"

"INDEFINITELY LONG. OUR PRESENT MAYOR WAS BORN IN 2998. THE AGE OF THE OLDEST CITY MAN OF WHOM WE HAVE ANY RECORD IS FIVE HUNDRED AND THIRTEEN YEARS, BUT IT IS STATISTICALLY DEFENSIBLE TO ASSUME THAT THERE ARE SEVERAL OLDER SPECIMENS, SINCE THE FIRST OF THE ANTIDEATH DRUGS WAS DISCOVERED IN THE YEAR 2018."

Antideath drugs! The dose was now entirely too big to swallow. It was all Chris could do to cling to the one microgram of it that seemed to have some meaning for him right now: that were he to live a long time—a very long time—he might some day find his way back home, no matter how far he had wandered in the meantime. All the rest would have to be thought through later. He said:

"I want to be a citizen."

"IT IS REQUIRED THAT WE INFORM YOU THAT YOU ARE PERMITTED TO CHANGE YOUR MIND UNTIL YOUR EIGHTEENTH BIRTHDAY, BUT THAT A DECISION TO BECOME A PASSENGER

MAY NOT THEREAFTER BE RESCINDED, EXCEPT BY SPECIAL ORDER OF THE MAYOR." A thin slot which Chris had not noticed until now suddenly spat out upon the banquette a long white card. "THIS IS YOUR CITY REGISTRATION, WHICH IS USED TO OBTAIN FOOD, CLOTHING, HOUSING AND OTHER NECESSITIES. WHEN IT IS REJECTED ON PRESENTATION, YOU WILL KNOW THAT THE GOODS OR SERVICES YOU HAVE CLAIMED HAVE BEEN DISALLOWED. THE CARD IS INDESTRUCTIBLE EXCEPT BY CERTAIN SPECIAL TECHNIQUES, BUT WE ADVISE YOU NOT TO LOSE IT, SINCE FOUR TO SIX HOURS WILL ELAPSE BEFORE IT CAN BE RETURNED TO YOU. IT IS PRESENTLY VALIDATED FOR ACCELERATED SCHOOLING. IF YOU HAVE NO FURTHER QUESTIONS, YOU MAY LEAVE."

The accelerated schooling to which the City Fathers had remanded Chris did not at first seem physically strenuous at all. In fact it seemed initially to be no more demanding than sleeping all day might be. (This to Chris was a Utopian notion; he had never had the opportunity to try sleeping as a career, and so had no idea how intolerably exhausting it is.)

The "schoolroom" was a large, gray, featureless chamber devoid of blackboard or desk; its only furniture consisted of a number of couches scattered about the floor. Nor were there any teachers; the only adults present were called monitors, and their duties appeared to be partly those of an usher, and partly those of a nurse, but none pertinent to teaching in any sense of the term Chris had ever encountered. They conducted you to your couch and helped you to fit over your head a bright metal helmet which had inside it what seemed to be hundreds of tiny, extremely sharp points which bit into your scalp just enough to make you nervous, but without enough pressure to break the skin. Once this gadget, which was called a toposcope, was adjusted to their satisfaction, the monitors left, and the room began to fill with the gray gas.

The gas was like a fog, except that it was dry and faintly aromatic, smelling rather like the dried leaves of mountain laurel that Bob had liked to add sparingly to rabbit stews. But like a thick fog, it made it impossible to see the rest of the room until the session was over, when it was sucked out with a subdued roar of blowers.

Thus Chris could never decide whether or not he actually slept while class was in session. The teaching technique, to be sure, was called hypnopaedia, an ancient word from still more ancient Greek roots which when translated literally meant "sleep-teaching." And, to be sure, it filled your head with strange voices and strange visions which were remarkably like dreams. Chris also suspected that the gray gas not only cut off his vision, but also his other senses; otherwise he should surely have heard such random sounds as the coughing of other students, the movements of the monitors, the whir of the ventilators, the occasional deep sounds of the city's drivers, and even the beating of his own heart; but none of these came through, or if they did, he did not afterwards have any memory of them. Yet the end result of all this was almost surely not true sleep, but simply a divorcing of his mind from every possible bodily distraction which might have come between him and his fullest attention to the visions and voices which were poured directly into his mind through the shining helmet of the toposcope.

It was easy to understand why no such distraction could be tolerated, for the torrent of facts that came from the memory cells of the City Fathers into the prickly helmet was overwhelming and merciless. More than once, Chris saw ex-Scrantonites, all of them older than he was, being supported by monitors out of the classroom at the end of a session in a state closely resembling the kind of epileptic fit called "petit mal" . . . nor were they ever allowed back on their couches again. He himself left the sessions in a curious state of wobbly, washed-out detachment which became more and more marked every day, despite the tumbler of restorative drink which was the standard antidote for the gray gas: a feeling of weakness which no amount of sleep seemed to make up for.

The drink tasted funny, furthermore, and besides, it made him sneeze. But on the day after he had refused it for the first time, the memory banks decanted a double dose of projective Riemannian geometry, and he awoke to find four monitors holding him down on the couch during the last throes of a classical Jacksonian seizure.

His education nearly stopped right there. Luckily, he had the sense to admit that he had skipped drinking the anticonvulsant drug the day before; and the records of the patterns of electrical activity of his brain which the toposcope had been taking continued to adjudge him a good risk. He was allowed back into the hall— and after that he was no longer in any doubt that learning can be harder physical labor than heaving a shovel.

The voices and the visions resumed swarming gleefully inside his aching head.

In retrospect, Chris found Okie history the least difficult subject to absorb, because the part of it dealing with the early years of the cities, and in particular with what had happened on Earth before the first of the cities had left the ground, was already familiar to him. Nevertheless he was now hearing it for the first time from the Okie point of view, which omitted great swatches which an Earthman would have considered important, and instead brought to the fore for study many events of which Chris had never heard but which obviously were essential for the understanding of how the cities had gone into space and prospered in it. It was, perhaps predictably, like seeing the past life of the Earth through the wrong end of a telescope.

As the memory banks told the story (without the pictures and sounds and other sensations, which, though they were so vivid as to become at once a part of Chris's immediate experience, could not possibly be reproduced in print), it went like this:

"The exploration of the solar system was at first primarily the province of the military, who alone could demand the enormous sums of money necessary for space travel under rocket power, which is essentially a brute-force method of propulsion directly dependent upon how much power is thrown away. The highest achievement of this phase was the construction of a research and observation station upon Proserpina II, the second satellite of the most remote of all the planets from Sol. Proserpina Station was begun in 2016; it was, however, still not completed when it was abandoned temporarily twenty-eight years later.

"The reasons for the abandonment of Proserpina Station and all other solar system colonies at this time may be found in the course of contemporary Terrestrial politics. Under the relentless pressure of competition from the USSR and its associated states, the Earth's Western culture had undertaken to support a permanent war economy, under the burden of which its traditional libertarian political institutions were steadily eroded away. By the beginning of the twenty-first century it was no longer realistically possible to see any difference between the rival cultures, although their outward forms of government continued to be called by different names. Both were police states in which the individual citizen had lost all right to juridical defense, and both operated under a totally controlled economy. In the West, the official term for this form of public policy was "anti-Communism"; in the East it was called "anti-Fascism," and both terms were heavily laden with mob emotion.

55

The facts of the matter, however, were that neither state was economically either fascist or communist, and that as economic systems neither fascism nor communism has ever been tried in recorded Terrestrial history.

"It was during this period that two Western research projects under the direction of the Alaskan senator Bliss Wagoner discovered the basic inventions upon which the second phase of space flight was to be based. The first of these was the Dillon-Wagoner gravitron-polarity generator, now known as the spindizzy, which was almost immediately developed into an interstellar drive. The second was ascomycin, the first of the anti-agathics, or death-postponing drugs. The first interstellar expedition was launched from the Jovian satellary system in 2021 under Wagoner's personal direction, although Wagoner himself was arrested and executed for his complicity in this 'treasonable' event. Though no record exists of the fate of this expedition, it is certain that it survived, since the second expedition, more than three hundred and fifty years later, found the planets of the stars of the local group well scattered with human beings speaking recognizable Terrestrial languages.

"At this time an attempt was made to settle the rivalry between the two power blocs by still another personal pact between their respective leaders, President MacHinery of the Western Common Market and Premier Erdsenov of the USSR. This took place in 2022, and the subsequent Cold Peace provided little incentive for space flight. In 2027 MacHinery was assassinated, and Erdsenov proclaimed himself premier and president of a United Earth; however, Erdsenov was himself assassinated in 2032. During this same year, an underground Western group calling itself the Hamiltonians succeeded in escaping from the solar system in a large number of small spindizzy-powered craft which they had built from funds collected secretly to finance a supposed new American revolution, thus leaving behind the vast majority of their followers. No survivors of the Hamiltonian exodus have thus far been found; they succeeded, however, in escaping the Terror, the worldwide program by which a united Earth government was actually established for the first time.

"One of the first acts of this government, now called the Bureaucratic State, was the banning in 2039 of spaceflight and all associated sciences. The existing colonies on the planets and satellites of the solar system were not evacuated home, but were simply cut off and abandoned. The consolidation of the State proceeded rapidly, and historians generally agree that the fall of the West must be dated no later than the year 2105. Thus began a period of systematic oppression and exploitation unmatched on Earth even by the worst decades of the Roman Empire.

"In the meantime the interstellar exiles continued to consolidate new planets and to jump from star to star. In 2289, one such expedition made its first contact with what proved to be a planet of the Vegan Tyranny, an interstellar culture which, we now know, had ruled most of this quadrant of the galaxy for eight to ten thousand years, and was still in the process of expanding. The Vegans were quick to see potential rivals even in these unorganized and badly supplied colonists, and made a concerted attempt to stamp out all the colonies. However, the distances involved were so vast that the first real engagement of the Vegan War, the battle of Altair, did not occur until 2310. The colonial forces were defeated and scattered, but not before inflicting sufficient damage to set back the Vegans timetable for razing the colonial planets—permanently, as it turned out.

"In 2375, the spindizzy was independently rediscovered on Earth and the Thorium Trust's Plant Number Eight used it to wrench its entire installation from off the ground and leave the Earth, using the plant as a self-contained spaceship. Other plants followed, and shortly thereafter, whole cities. Many of these were driven to leave as much by the permanent depression which had settled over the Earth as by the long-established political repressions of the Bureaucratic State. These escaping cities quickly found the earlier Earth colonies among the nearby stars, to which they provided badly needed industrial strength, and with whom they joined forces against Vega. The outcome was both triumphant and shameful. In 2394 one of the escaping cities, Gravitogorsk-Mars, now calling itself the Interstellar Master Traders, was responsible for the sacking of the new Earth colony on Thor V; this act of ferocity earned for them the nickname of 'the Mad Dogs,' but it gradually became a model for dealing with Vegan planets. The capital world of the Tyranny, Vega II, was invested in 2413 by a number of armed cities, including IMT, whose task it was to destroy the many orbital forts surrounding the planet, and by the Third Colonial Navy under Admiral Alois Hrunta, who was charged with occupying Vega II in the event of its surrender. Instead, Admiral Hrunta scorched the planet completely, and led the Third Navy off into an uncharted quadrant with the intention of founding his own interstellar empire. In 2451 the colonial court found him guilty *in absentia* of atrocities and attempted genocide, and an attempt to bring him to justice culminated in 2464 in the battle of BD 40° 4048', which was destructive but completely indecisive for both sides. The same year Alois Hrunta declared himself Emperor of Space.

"The Exodus of Earth's industrial power had by now become so marked that the Bureaucratic State no longer had a productive base upon which to rest, and it is generally agreed that it collapsed in 2522. In the same year there began the police interregnum, a limited government deriving its powers from a loose confederation based roughly upon the ancient United Nations, but without sufficient popular base or industrial support to control the economy. Realizing, however, that the only hope for the restoration of economic health to Earth lay in the colonists and the free cities, the confederation proclaimed an amnesty for everyone in space, and at the same time instituted a limited but systematic program for the policing of those nomad cities which had begun to prey upon colony planets or upon each other.

"The confederation is still the only operative government in this arm of the galaxy. The poisoning of Alois Hrunta in 3089 was followed by the rapid Balkanization of the Hruntan Empire, which was never even at its best highly cohesive, and although there is a present self-styled Emperor of Space, Arpad Hrunta, his realm does not appear to be of any importance. Effectively, today, law and order in Arm II are provided by the Earth police, and its economy is supported by the migrant cities. Both systems are haphazard and inefficient, and often operate at cross purposes.

"It is impossible to predict when better methods will emerge, or what they will be."

5

"BOY, YOU ARE DUMB!"

While the memory cells chattered and called up dreams, the immense city soared outward among the stars, at what seemed like a breakneck pace after the tentative first explorations of Scranton within the local group. The streets were thronged 24 hours a day with myriads of people hurrying on unimaginable errands; and in addition to the constant flitting of Tin Cabs, there was often the distant but edgy roar of subway trains coursing through tunnels bored through the very granite keel of the city. All of this activity seemed purposeful and even cheerful, but it was also extremely bewildering.

Chris's schooling left him very little time to explore it. Not all of his education was machine education, either, for, as he slowly realized, no one really *learns* anything through hypnopaedia; machine teaching at its best enables the student to accumulate nothing better than facts; it does not show how to tie them together, let alone how to do something with them. To train the intelligence—not just the memory—a real human tutor is required.

The one assigned to Chris, a stocky, fierce, white-haired woman named Dr. Helena Braziller, was far and away the best teacher Chris had ever encountered in his life—and far and away the worst taskmaster. The City

Fathers wore him out only by taxing his memory; whereas Dr. Braziller made him *work*.

"The fundamental equation of the Blackett-Dirac scholium reads as follows:

$$P = \frac{BG^{\frac{1}{2}}U}{2C}$$

where P is magnetic moment, U is angular momentum, C and G have their usual values, and B is a constant with the value 0.25 approximately. A first transform of this identity gives:

$$G = \left(\frac{2PC}{BU}\right)^2$$

which is the usual shorthand form of the primary spin-dizzy equation, called the Locke Derivation. Blackett, Dirac and Locke all assumed that it would hold true for large bodies, such as gas-giant planets and suns. Show on the blackboard by dimensional analysis why this assumption is invalid."

As far as Chris was concerned, the answer could have been much more simply arrived at; Dr. Braziller could just have told him that this relationship between gravitation and the spin of a body applied only to electrons and other submicroscopic objects, and disappeared, for all practical purposes, in the world of the macrocosm; but that was not her way. Had she only told him that, it would have come into his mind as a fact like any other fact—for instance, like the facts that the memory cells of the City Fathers were constantly pouring into his ears and eyes—but by her lights he would not have understood it. She wanted him to repeat not only the original reasoning of Blackett, Dirac and Locke, but to see for himself, not just because she told him so, where they had gone astray, and hence why a natural law which had first been proposed in the gas-lit, almost pre-historic year of 1891, and was precisely formulated as the Lande Factor in 1940, nevertheless failed to lift so much as a grain of sand off the Earth until the year 2019.

"But Dr. Braziller, why isn't it enough to see that they made a mistake? We know that now. Why repeat it?"

"Because that's what all these great men have labored toward: so that you could do it right, yourself. Up until about the thirteenth century, nobody in the world except a few dedicated scholars could do long division; then Fibonacci introduced Arabic numbers to the West. Now, any idiot can do what it took a great mind to do in those days. Are you going to complain that because Fibonacci found a better way to do long division, you shouldn't be required to learn why it's better? Or that because a great inventor like Locke didn't understand dimensional analysis, you should be allowed to be just as ignorant, after all these years? They spent their lives making things simple for you that were enormously difficult for them, and until you understand the difficulties, you can't possibly understand the simplifications. Go back to the blackboard and try again."

Being in a "live" class had its compensations, though; and one of these was Piggy Kingston-Throop. Piggy—his real name was George, but nobody ever called him that, not even Dr. Braziller—was not much of a prize as a friend and companion, but he was the only member of the small class who was exactly Chris's age; all the others were much younger. From this Chris deduced that Piggy was not a student, which turned out to be true.

Piggy seemed glad enough to encounter someone who was as retarded as he was, whatever the reasons, and who knew less than he did about a great many subjects which were commonplaces to him. And in many ways he was quite a pleasant sort of fellow: blond, plump and affable, with a ready wit and a tendency to be unimpressed by almost everything that other people considered important. In this last, he made a particularly good foil for Chris, who in his ignorance and in the strangeness of his situation often could not help but be earnest to the point of grimness over what later turned out to be trivia.

Not that Chris allowed these differences over value judgments always to be resolved in Piggy's favor; they quarreled over them almost from the beginning. The first of these tangles, which soon proved to be a model for the others, involved the subject of the antiagathic drugs.

"You're going to be a citizen, aren't you, Piggy?"

"Oh, sure. I'm all set."

"I wish I were. My trouble is, I don't even know what I want to do—let alone what I'm good at."

Piggy turned and stared at him. They had paused on the way from school on the Tudor Tower Place bridge leading over 42nd Street. Long ago, the view from here across First Avenue to the East River had been blocked by the UN Building, but that had been demolished during the Terror, and there was nothing to mark where it had stood but a plaza; and on the far side of that, starry space itself.

"What do you mean, do?" Piggy said. "Oh, maybe you'll have a little trouble, what with not having been born here. But there's ways around that. Don't believe everything they tell you."

Like many of the things Piggy said, fully 80 per cent of this speech meant nothing to Chris. In self-defense, he could do nothing but answer the question. "You know all this better than I do. But the laws do say pretty clearly that a man has to be good for something before he's allowed to become a citizen and be started on the drug treatments. Let's see; there are supposed to be three ways to go about it; and I ought to have them straight, because I just had them put into my head a few days ago."

He concentrated a moment. He had discovered a useful trick for dredging up the information which had been implanted in his mind from the memory cells: If he half closed his eyes and imagined the gray gas, in a moment he would begin to feel, at least in retrospect, the same somnolence under which the original facts had been imparted, and they would come back in very much the same words. It worked equally well this time; almost at once, he heard his own voice saying, in a curious monotone imitation of the City Fathers:

"'There are three general qualifications for citizenship. They are: (1) Display of some obviously useful talent, such as computer programming, administration, or another gift worth retaining, as opposed to depending upon the accidents of birth to provide new such men for each succeeding generation; (2) a demonstrable bent toward any intellectual field, including scientific research, the arts and philosophy, since in these fields one lifetime is seldom enough to attain masterhood, let alone put it to the best use; and (3) passage of the Citizenship Tests, which are designed to reveal reserves and potentials in the late-maturing eighteen-year-old whose achievement record is unimpressive.' No matter how you slice it, it doesn't sound easy!"

That's only what the City Fathers say, Piggy said scornfully. "What do they know about it? They're only a bunch of machines. They don't know anything about people. Those rules don't even make sense."

"They make sense to me," Chris objected. "It's a cinch the antiagathics can't be given to everybody—from what I hear, they're scarcer than germanium. On Scranton, the big boss wouldn't even allow them to be mentioned in public. So there's got to be *some* way of picking who gets them and who doesn't."

"Why?"

"Why? Well, to begin with, because a city is like an island—an island in the middle of the biggest ocean you can think of, and then some. Nobody can get on, and nobody can get off, except for a couple of guys now and then. If everybody gets this drug and lives forever, pretty soon the place is going to be so crowded that we'll all be standing on each other's feet."

"Ah, cut it out. Look around you. Are *we* all standing on each other's feet?"

"No, but that's because the drugs are restricted, and because not everybody's allowed to have children, either. For that matter, look at you, Piggy—your father and your mother are both big wheels on this town, but you're an only child, and furthermore, the first one they've been allowed to have in a hundred and fifty years."

"Leave them out of this," Piggy growled. "They didn't play their cards right, I'll tell you that. But that's none of your business."

"All right. Take me, then. Unless I turn out to be good for something before I'm eighteen—and I can't think what it would be—I won't be a citizen and I won't get the drugs. Or even if I do get to be a citizen, say by passing the Tests, I'll still have to prove myself useful stock before I'm allowed to have even one kid of my own. That's just the way it has to be when the population has to be kept stable; it's simple economics, Piggy, and there's a subject I think I know something about."

Piggy spat reflectively over the railing, though it was hard to tell whether or not he was expressing an opinion, and if so, whether it referred to economics alone or to the entire argument. "All right, then," he said. "Suppose you get the drugs, and they let you have a kid. Why shouldn't they give the kid the drugs too?"

"Why should they, unless he qualifies?"

"Boy, you *are* dumb! That's what the Citizenship

Tests are for, can't you see that? They're an out—an escape hatch, a dodge—and that's all they are. If you don't get in any other way, you get in that way. At least you do if you've got any sort of connections. If you're a nobody, maybe the City Fathers rig the Tests against you—that's likely enough. But if you're a somebody, they're not going to be too tough. If they are, my father can fix their wagon—he programs 'em. But either way, there's no way to study for the Tests, so they're obviously a sell."

Chris was shaken, but he said doggedly: "But they're not supposed to be that kind of test at all. I mean, they're not supposed to show whether or not you're good at dimensional analysis, or history, or some other subject. They're supposed to show up gifts that you were born with, not anything that you got through schooling or training."

"Spindizzy whistle. A test you can't study for is a test you can't pass unless it's rigged—otherwise it doesn't make any sense at all. Listen, Red, if you're so sold on this idea that everybody who gets to take the drugs has to be a big brain, what about the guardian they handed you over to? He's got no kids of his own, and he's nothing but a cop . . . but he's almost as old as the Mayor!"

Up to now, Chris had felt vaguely that he had been holding his own; but this was like a blow in the face.

Chris had originally been alarmed to find that his ID card assigned him lodgings with a family, and horrified when the assignment number turned out to belong to Sgt. Anderson. His first few weeks in the Andersons' apartment—it was in the part of the city once called Chelsea—were prickly with suspicion, disguised poorly by as much formality as his social inexperience would allow.

It soon became impossible, however, to continue believing that the perimeter sergeant was an ogre; and his wife, Carla, was as warm and gracious a woman as Chris had ever met. They were childless, and could not have welcomed Chris more whole-heartedly had he been one of their own. Furthermore, as the City Fathers had of course calculated, Anderson was the ideal guardian for a brand-new young passenger, for few people, even the Mayor, knew the city better.

He was, in fact, considerably more than a cop, for the city's police force was also its defense force—and its Marines, should the need for a raid or a boarding party ever arise. Technically, there were many men on the force who were superior to the perimeter sergeant, but Anderson and one counterpart, a dark taciturn man named Dulany, headed picked squads and were nearly independent of the rest of the police, reporting directly to Mayor Amalfi.

It was this fact which opened the first line of friendly communication between Chris and his guardian. He had not yet even seen Amalfi with his own eyes. Although everyone in the city spoke of him as if they knew him personally, here at last was one man who really did, and saw him several times a week. Chris was unable to restrain his curiosity.

"Well, that's just the way people talk, Chris. Actually hardly anyone sees much of Amalfi; he's got too much to do. But he's been in charge here a long time and he's good at his job; people feel that he's their friend because they trust him."

"But what is he *like?*"

"He's complicated—but then most people are complicated. I guess the word I'm groping for is 'devious.' He sees connections between events that nobody else sees. He sizes up a situation like a man looking at a coat for the one thread that'll make the whole thing unravel. He has to—he's too burdened to deal with things on a stitch-by-stitch basis. In my opinion he's killing himself with overwork as it is."

It was to this point that Chris returned after his up-setting argument with Piggy. "Sergeant, the other day you said that the Mayor was killing himself with over-work. But the City Fathers told me he's several centuries old. On the drugs, he ought to live forever, isn't that so?"

"Absolutely not," Anderson said emphatically. "*Nobody* can live forever. Sooner or later, there'd be an accident, for one thing. And strictly speaking, the drugs aren't a 'cure' for death anyhow. Do you know how they work?"

"No," Chris admitted. "School hasn't covered them yet."

"Well, the memory banks can give you the details—I've probably forgotten most of them. But generally, there are several antiagathics, and each one does a dif-ferent job. The main one, ascomycin, stirs up a kind of tissue in the body called the reticulo-endothelial system —the white blood corpuscles are a part of it—to give you what's called 'nonspecific immunity.' What that means is that for about the next seventy years, you can't catch any infectious disease. At the end of that time you get another shot, and so on. The stuff isn't an antibiotic, as the name suggests, but an endotoxin fraction—a complex organic sugar called a mannose; it got its name from the fact that it's produced by fermentation, as antibiotics are.

"Another is TATP—triacetyltriparanol. What this does is inhibit the synthesis in the body of a fatty stuff called cholesterol; otherwise it collects in the arteries and causes strokes, apoplexy, high blood pressure and so on. This drug has to be taken every day, because the body goes right on trying to make cholesterol every day."

"Doesn't that mean that it's good for something?" Chris objected tentatively.

"Cholesterol? Sure it is. It's absolutely essential in the development of a fetus, so women have to lay off

TATP while they're carrying a child. But it's of no use to men—and men are far more susceptible to circulatory diseases than women.

"There are still two more antiagathics in use now, but they're minor; one, for instance, blocks the synthesis of the hormone of sleep, which again is essential in pregnancy but a thundering nuisance otherwise; that one was originally found in the blood of ruminant animals like cows, whose plumbing is so defective that they'd die if they lay down."

"You mean you *never sleep?*"

"Haven't got the time for it," Anderson said gravely. "Or the need any longer, thank goodness. But ascomycin and TATP between them prevent the two underlying major causes of death: heart diseases and infections. If you prevent those alone, you extend the average lifetime by at least two centuries.

"But death is still inevitable, Chris. If there isn't an accident, there may be cancer, which we can't prevent yet—oh, ascomycin attacks tumors so strongly that cancer doesn't kill people any longer, in fact the drug even offers quite a lot of protection against hard radiation; but cancer can still make life so agonizing that death is the only humane treatment. Or a man can die of starvation, or of being unable to get the antiagathics. Or he can die of a bullet—or of overwork. We live long lives in the cities, sure; *but there is no such thing as immortality.* It's as mythical as the unicorn. Not even the universe itself is going to last forever."

This, at last, was the opportunity Chris had been hoping for, though he still hardly knew how to grasp it.

"Are—are the drugs ever stopped, once a man's been made a citizen?"

"Deliberately? I've never heard of such a case," Anderson said, frowning. "Not on our town. If the City Fathers want a man dead, they shoot him. Why let him linger for the rest of his seventy-year stanza? That would be outrageously cruel. What would be the reason for such a procedure?"

"Well, no tests are foolproof. I mean, supposing they make a man a citizen, and then discover that he really isn't—uh—as big a genius as they thought he was?"

The perimeter sergeant looked at Chris narrowly, and there was quite a long silence, during which Chris could clearly hear the pulsing of his own blood in his temples. At last Anderson said slowly:

"I see. It sounds to me like somebody's been feeding you spindizzy whistle. Chris, if only geniuses could become citizens, how long do you think a city could last? The place'd be depopulated in one crossing. That isn't how it works at all. The whole reason for the drugs is to save skills—and it doesn't matter one bit what the skills are. All that matters is whether or not it would be logical to keep a man on, rather than training a new one every four or five decades.

"Take me for an example, Chris. I'm nobody's genius; I'm only a boss cop. But I'm good at my job, good enough so that the City Fathers didn't see any reason to bother raising and training another one from the next generation; they kept this one, which is me; but a cop is, all the same, all I am. Why not? It suits me, I like the work, and when Amalfi needs a boss cop he calls me or Dulany—not any officer on the force, because none of them have the scores of years of experience at this particular job that we do under their belts. When the Mayor wants a perimeter sergeant he calls me; when he wants a boarding squad he calls Dulany; and when he wants a specific genius, he calls a genius. There's one of everything on board this town—partly because it's so big—and so long as the system works, no need for more than one. Or more than X, X being whatever number you need."

Chris grinned. "You seemed to remember the details all right."

"I remembered them all," Anderson admitted. "Or all that they gave me. Once the City Fathers put a thing into your head, it's hard to get rid of."

As he spoke, there was a pure fluting sound, like a brief tune, somewhere in the apartment. The perimeter sergeant's heavy head tipped up; then he, too, grinned.

"We're about to have a demonstration," he said. He was obviously pleased. He touched a button on the arm of his chair.

"Anderson?" a heavy voice said. Chris thought instantly that the father bear in the ancient myth of Goldilocks must have sounded much like that.

"Yes—Here, sir."

"We're coming up on a contract. It looks fairly good to me and the City Fathers, and I'm about to sign it. Better come up here and familiarize yourself with the terms, just in case: This'll be a rough one, Joel."

"Right away." Anderson touched the button, and his grin became broader and more boyish than ever.

"The Mayor!" Chris burst out.

"Yep."

"But what did he mean?"

"That he's found some work for us to do. Unless there's a hitch, we should be landing in just a few days."

6

A PLANET CALLED HEAVEN

Nothing could be seen of Heaven from the air. As the city descended cautiously, the spindizzy field became completely outlined as a bubble of boiling black clouds, glaring with blue-green sheets and slashes of lightning, and awash with streams of sleet and rain. At lower altitude the sleet disappeared, but the rain increased.

After so many months of starlit skies and passing suns, the grumbling, closed-in darkness was oppressive, even alarming. Sitting with Piggy on an old pier at the foot of Gansevoort Street, from which Herman Melville had sailed into the distant South Sea marvels of *Typee*, *Omoo* and *Mardi*, Chris stared at the globe of thunder around the city as nervously as though he had never seen weather before. Piggy, for once, was in no better shape, for he never *had* seen weather before; this was New York's first planetfall since he had been born.

How Amalfi could see where he was going was hard to imagine; but the city continued to go down anyhow; it had a contract with Heaven, and work was work. Besides, there would have been no point in waiting for the storms to clear away. It was always and everywhere like this on Heaven, except when it was worse. The settlers said so.

"Wow!" Chris said, for the twelfth or thirteenth time.

"What a blitzkrieg of a storm! Look at *that!* How far up are we still, Piggy?"

"How should I know?"

"D'you think Amalfi knows? I mean really knows?"

"Sure, he knows," Piggy said miserably. "He always does the tough landings. He never misses."

WHAM!

For a second the whole sphere of the spindizzy field seemed to be crawling with electric fire. The noise was enormous and bounded back again and again from the concrete sides of the towers behind them. It had never occurred to Chris that a field which could protect a whole city from the hard radiation, the hard stones and the hard vacuum of space might pass noise when there was air outside it as well as inside—but it surely did. The descent already seemed to have been going on forever.

After a while, Chris found that he was beginning to enjoy it. Between thunder rolls, he shouted maliciously:

"He must be flying sidewise this time. But he's lost."

"What do you know about it? Shut up."

"*I've* seen thunderstorms. You know what? We're going to be up here forever. Sailing under a curse, like IMT." The sky lit. *WHAM!* "Hey, what a beauty!"

"If you don't shut up," Piggy said with desperate grimness, "I'm going to poke you right in the snoot."

This was hardly a very grave threat, for although Piggy outweighed Chris by some twenty pounds, most of it was blubber. Amid the excitement of the storm Chris almost made the mistake of laughing at him; but at the same instant, he felt the boards of the ancient pier begin to shudder beneath them to the tramp of steel boots. Startled, he looked back over his shoulder, and then jumped up.

Twenty men in full space armor were behind them, faceless and bristling, like a phalanx of giant robots. One of them came forward, making the planks of the pier groan and squeal under the weight, and suddenly spoke to him.

The voice was blarey and metallic, as though the gain had been turned up in order to shout across acres of ground and through cannonades of thunder, but Chris had no difficulty in recognizing it. The man in the armor was his guardian.

"CHRIS!" The volume of sound suddenly went down a little. "Chris, what are you doing here? And Kingston-Throop's kid! Piggy, you ought to know better than this. We're landing in twenty minutes—and this is a sally port. Beat it—both of you."

"We were only looking," Piggy said defiantly. "We can look if we want."

"I've got no time to argue. Are you going or not?"

Chris pulled at Piggy's elbow. "Come on, Piggy. What's the sense of being in the way?"

"Let go. I'm not in the way. They can walk right by me. I don't have to go just because he says so. He's not *my* guardian—he's only a cop."

A steel arm reached out, and steel pincers opened at the end of it. "Give me your card," Anderson's voice said harshly. "I'll let you know later what you're charged with. If you won't move now, I'll assign two men to move you—though I can't spare the men, and when that winds up on your card you may spend the rest of one lifetime wishing it hadn't."

"Oh, all right. Don't throw your weight around. I'm going."

The bulbous steel arm remained stiffly extended, the pincers menacingly open. "I want the card."

"I said I was going!"

"Then go."

Piggy broke and ran. After a puzzled look at the armored figure of his guardian, Chris followed, dodging around and through the massive blue-steel statues standing impassively along almost the whole length of the pier.

Piggy had already vanished. As Chris ran for home, his mind full of bewilderment, the city grounded in a fanfare of lightning bolts.

Unfortunately, so far as Chris was concerned the City Fathers took no notice of the landing: his schooling went on regardless, so that he got only the most confused picture of what was going on. Though the municipal pipeline, WNYC, had five-minute news bulletins on tap every hour for anyone who wanted to dial into them, decades of the uneventfulness of interstellar travel had reduced the WNYC news bureau to a state of vestigial ineptitude—the pipeline's only remaining real function was the broadcasting of the city's inexhaustible library of music and drama; Chris suspected that most of the citizens found the newscasts almost as dim-witted and uninformative as he did. What little meaningful information he was able to garner, he got from Sgt. Anderson, and that was not very much, for the perimeter sergeant was hardly ever home now; he was too busy consolidating the beachhead on Heaven. Nevertheless, Chris picked up a few fragments, mostly from conversations between the sergeant and Carla:

"What they want us to do is to help them industrialize the planet. It sounds easy, but the kicker is that their social setup is feudal—the sixty-six thousand people they call the Elect are actually only free landholders or franklins, and below *them* there's a huge number of serfs—nobody's ever bothered to count them. The Archangels want it to stay that way even after they've got their heavy industries established."

"It sounds impossible," Carla said.

"It is impossible, as they'll find out when we've finished the job. But that's exactly the trouble. We're not allowed to change planets' social systems, but we

75

can't complete this contract without starting a revolution —a long, slow one, sure, but a revolution all the same. And when the cops come here afterward and find that out, we'll have a Violation to answer for."

Carla laughed musically. "The cops! My dear, is that still a three-letter word for you? What else are you? How many more centuries is it going to take you to get used to it?"

"You know what I mean," Anderson said, frowning. "So all right, I'm a cop. But I'm not an Earth cop, I'm a *city* cop, and that makes all the difference. Well, we'll see. What's for lunch? I've got to go in half an hour."

The storm, as predicted, went on all the time. When he had the chance, Chris watched the machinery being uncrated and readied, and followed it to the docks at the working perimeter of the city, beyond which always bobbed and crawled a swarm of the glowing swamp vehicles of the colonists of Heaven. Though these came in all sizes, they were all essentially of the same design: a fat cylinder of some transparent cladding, ribbed with metal, provided on both sides with caterpillar treads bearing cleats so large that they could also serve as paddles where the going underfoot became especially sloppy. The shell was airtight, for buoyancy, but Chris was sure that the vessel could make little or no headway afloat, even if it were equipped somewhere with a screw propeller; under those circumstances it probably could do no more than try to maintain its position as best it could while it radioed for help. It was certainly well studded with antennae. Mainly, it seemed to be designed to shed water, rather than to swim in it.

How could any sort of industry be possible under these soggy conditions? He could not imagine how even an agricultural society could survive amidst these perpetual torrents, especially since there was very little land area above water on the planet. But then he recalled a little of the history of the colonization of Venus, which had presented somewhat similar problems. There, farming eventually had been taken beneath the sea; but even that needed an abundance of energy, and besides, the people of Heaven hadn't even gotten that far—they seemed to be living mostly on fish and mudweed.

He listened as closely as possible to the conversations of the colonists on the docks—not the conversations in English with the Okies, which were technical and unrevealing, but what the colonists said to each other in their own language. This was a gluey variant of Russian, the now dead Universal language of deep space, which the memory cells had been cramming into Chris's head at a cruel rate almost since the beginning of his city education. It was a brute of a language to master, especially on board a town where it was very seldom used, and perhaps for this reason the colonists, though mostly they were circumspect even in their private conversations, did not really seem to believe that the Okies spoke it; their very possession of it assured them that their history was safely pre-Okie. Quite certainly it never occurred to them that it might be understood, however imperfectly, by a teen-age boy standing about the quaysides gawping at their powerboats.

Between these eavesdroppings and the increasingly rare visits home of this guardian, Chris gradually built up a fuzzy picture of what the colonists seemed to want. As a citizen, he could have asked the City Fathers directly for the text of the contract, but access to this was denied to passengers. In general, however, he gathered that the Archangels proposed to establish an economy like that of Venus, complete with undersea farming and herding, with the aid of broadcast power of the kind that kept the city's Tin Cabs in the air. The Okies were to do the excavating in the shifting, soaking terrain, and were to build the generator-transmitter station involved. They were also to use city facilities to refine the necessary power metals, chiefly thorium, of which Heaven had an abundance beyond its ability to process. After the economy was revamped, the Archangels hoped to have their own refineries, and to sell the pure stuffs to other planets. Curiously, they also had enough germanium to be willing to pay for the job in this metal, although it too was notoriously difficult to refine; this was fortunate for them, since without any present interstellar trade, they were woefully short of Oc Dollars.

Once the whole operation had rumbled and sloshed out into the field and was swallowed up in the enveloping, eternal storm, Sgt. Anderson's absences became prolonged, and the number of colonists to be found on the docks also diminished sharply. Now there were only a few of the swamp vehicles—inexplicably called swan boats—to be seen at the end of each day, when Chris was released from school, and these were mostly small craft whose owners were engaged in dickering with individual Okies for off-planet curios to give to their ladies. This commerce also was bogging down rather rapidly, for the single citizen had no use for money, and the lords and franklins of Heaven had few goods to barter. Soon the flow of information available to Chris had almost stopped, frustrating him intensely.

In this extremity he had an inspiration. He still carried with him a small, cheap clasp knife with a tiny compass embedded in its handle, the last of the exceedingly few gifts his father had ever been able to give him; perhaps it would have status here as an off-planet curio. When the notion first occurred to him, he rejected it with distress at even having thought of it—but when first Sgt. Dulany, and then his own guardian, were officially posted on the "Missing" list, he hesitated no longer. His only remaining doubt was whether or not the compass would work here, amid so much electrical activity (but then it had never worked very well on Earth, either).

He waited until he saw the lord of a six-man swan boat stalking disappointedly away from a deal he had been unable to close, and then approached him with the knife outstretched on his palm.

"*Gospodin—*"

The man, a huge burly fellow with a face like one of the eternal thunderclouds of his planet, stopped in his tracks and looked down. "Boy? Did you speak?"

"Yes sir. With your permission, I have here useful tool, earthly in origin. Would my lord care to examine?"

"But you speak our language," the man said, still frowning. He took the knife abstractedly; it was plain that he was interested, but Chris's stumbling Russian seemed to interest him more. "How is that?"

"By listening, lord. It is very hard, but I am trying. Please see object, it is from Earth, from *kolkhoz* of Pennsylvania. Genuine antique, touched once by human hands in factory."

"Well, well. How does it work?"

Chris showed him how to pry out the two blades, but his attempts to explain the compass were dismissed with a brusque gesture. Either his command of the language was insufficient to make the matter clear, or the lord already had recognized that such a thing would be useless in the lightning-stitched ether of Heaven.

"Hmm. Sleazy, to be sure, but perhaps my lady would like it for her charm-necklace. What do you ask for it?"

"Lord, I would like to drive your swan boat one time, one distance. I ask no more."

The colonist stared at him for a long moment, and then burst into deep guffaws of laughter. "Come along, come along," he said when he had recovered a little. "Sharp traders, you tramps, but this is the best story yet —I'll be telling it for years! Come along—you have a bargain."

Still chortling, he led the way to the dock, where they were both stopped by a perimeter cop who recognized Chris. Between them, the boy and the lord explained the bargain, and the Okie guard dubiously allowed Chris to board the swan boat.

In the forward cabin of the bobbing cylinder, two other colonists confronted them at once, wearing expressions at once nervous and angry, but the owner shushed them with a swift slash of one hand. He still seemed to be highly amused.

"It's only an infant. It traded me a bangle to learn how to mush the boat about. There's nothing to that. Go on aft; I'll join you in a minute."

To judge by their expressions, the other two still disapproved, but they took orders. The big man sat Chris down in a bucket seat before the broad front window and showed him how to grasp the two handles, one on each side of the half-circle of the control wheel, which were the throttles of the vehicle.

"It's not enough simply to turn the wheel, because you must also deliver power to one tread or the other. To do that, you push the handle forward or back, to speed the treads or slow them down. Past the red mark here, the tread will reverse. If you're not getting any traction, tilt the whole wheel forward on its column; that blows the tanks and allows the boat to settle in the mud. When the ground gets harder, the boat will of course climb up by itself and that will start the pumps; as the pressure in the tanks rises, the steering column tilts back to its original position automatically. Understand me so far?"

"But can I try?"

"Well, I suppose so. Yes. I have some talking to do abaft. Let me back the craft away from the pier, and then you can try crawling in a circle just outside the perimeter. Make sure you can always see your city beacon there."

"Let me back it up, lord?" Chris said urgently.

"All right," the big man said with amused indulgence. "But don't be rough with it. Gently back of the red line on both throttles. That's it. Not so fast. Gently! Now into neutral on the left. That's it; see how it turns around?"

There was a shout from somewhere in the rear of the vessel, to which the big man responded with a tremendously rapid burst of speech, only a few words of which were intelligible to Chris. "I have to leave for a few minutes," he added. "Remember, don't try anything tricky, and don't lose sight of the beacon."

"No, lord."

As the boat's owner left the cabin, Chris caught a few more words, amusedly beginning to relate the story of the dock boy who had picked up a few stammering words of the language and immediately had decided that he was a pilot; then the voices dwindled to a blurred murmur. Chris spent the next few minutes testing the controls of the boat in small jerks and spurts, being as inexpert about it as he could manage, although the machine was really not difficult to master. Then, as directed, he set it to crawling in a fixed circle, counter-clockwise, left the bucket seat, and edged his way back to the door leading to the next chamber.

He had no idea what it was that he expected to overhear—he was simply avid for more information, to relieve the recent famine. He was certainly unprepared for what he got.

The men were talking in a rapid patois which differed sharply from the form of the Universal Language which the memory cells had been teaching him, but many phrases were clear and distinct:

". . . can't be done without keeping the city, that's all there is to it."

". . . Disable it? . . . Don't even have a blueprint of the machinery, let alone a map."

"That can come later, after we've occupied . . . We've

81

got thousands of commoners to throw away, but the defenses—It's essential first to immobilize their Huacu, or whatever they call it here. We can't afford to fight on their terms."

"Then what's the problem? We've got their two chief generals for hostages. We can hold them forever if necessary . . . Don't even know the name of Castle Wolfwhip, let alone where it—"

There the conversation ended abruptly. With a grinding thump, the swan boat hit something and began clumsily to try to climb it. Chris was thrown to the deck, and on the other side of the doorway there was the sound of scrambling and of angry shouting. Then that too was cut off as the bulkhead swung to, of its own inertia.

Fighting to regain his balance against the blind lurching of the boat, Chris scrambled up, and dogged the bulkhead tightly closed all the way around. Was there any way to lock it, too? Yes, there was a big bolt that could be thrown which would hold the whole series of dogs in place, provided that it could not be unbolted from the other side. Well, he'd have to take his chances on that, though a fat padlock to complete the job would have made him feel more comfortable. Then, he clambered up the tilted, pitching deck to the control seat.

The boat had been doing its best to travel in a circle, but Chris had failed to realize that mud is a shifting, inexact sort of medium in which to turn a machine loose. The circle had been precessing, and the boat had run head-on into a dock. Okie cops were running toward it.

Chris reversed both engines, backing away from the city as rapidly as the boat would go, but that was not half as fast as he would have liked. Then he switched the vehicle around, end for end, and set it to whining and sliding squarely into the teeth of the storm, aiming it for the pip on the cross hairs which showed on the control board as its homing signal.

Where that might wind him up, he had no idea. He could only hope that it might be Castle Wolfwhip, and that he would find Anderson and Dulany there—and that the six furious colonists in back of the locked bulkhead would not be able to burn their way out before he got there.

7

WHY NOT TO KEEP DEMONS

Before the swan boat had been on its slobbering way outward for more than five minutes, the sodium-yellow glare of the city's dockside beacon dimmed and vanished as swiftly as if it had been snuffed out. Except for his prisoners, whom he was trying to ignore, Chris was alone in the shell of the boat, like a chick in an egg, with nothing for company but the unfamiliar instruments, the grunting of the engines, and the flash and crash of the eternal storm.

He studied the control board intently, but it told him very little that he did not already know. All the lettering on and around the instruments was in the Cyrillic alphabet—and although the City Fathers expected citizens to be able to speak the Universal Language, up to now they had given Chris not even a first lesson in how to read it. Even so obvious a device as the swan boat's radio set was incomprehensible to him in detail; after a brief study, he gave up all hope of finding the city's master frequency and calling for pursuit and aid. He could not even decide whether it was an AFM or a PM tuner, let alone read the calibrations on the dial.

Nevertheless he urgently needed to signal. Above all, he needed to let the city know the details, fragmentary though they were, of the plotting that he had overheard. Running away with the plotters in their own swan boat had been an impulse of desperation, which he was already beginning more and more to regret. If only he had managed somehow to get back on shore, and told somebody in Amalfi's office what he had learned, pronto!

But the question was, would they have listened, or believed him if they had? Nobody who was anybody aboard the city seemed to want to bother with youngsters until they had become citizens; the adults were all too old, somehow, to be even approachable—and for that matter citizens paid very little attention to passengers of any age.

Of course, Chris could have told the City Fathers what he knew, easily enough—but everything that was told the City Fathers went into the memory cells, which was the equivalent of putting it in dead storage. The City Fathers never took action on what they knew, or even volunteered information, unless directed; otherwise they only held it until it was asked for, which might take centuries.

In any event the die was cast. Now he also needed someone in the city to know where he was going, and to follow him. But among the glittering, enigmatic instruments before him he could find no way to bring that about, nor did he in fact know even vaguely how the city might chase after him if it did know what his situation was. The Tin Cabs operated upon broadcast power which faded out at the city's perimeter, and to the best of Chris's knowledge, the city had no ground vehicles capable of coping with shifting, ambiguous, invisible terrain of this kind. Somewhere in storage, true, it did have a limited number of larger military aircraft, but how could you fly one of them in this region of perpetual storm? And even if you could, what would you look for, in a world where even the largest villages and castles produced and consumed so little power that detecting instruments would be unable to differentiate a city from a random splatter of lightning bolts?

The swan boat churned onward single-mindedly. After a while, Chris noticed that it had been at least several minutes since he had had to apply corrections in order to keep the green pip on the cross hairs. Experimentally, he let go of the controls entirely. The pip stayed centered. Some signal—perhaps simply his keeping the pip centered for a given length of time—had cut in an automatic pilot.

That was a help, in a way, but it deprived him of anything to do but worry, and added a new worry to the list: How could he cut the autopilot *out* of the circuit if he needed to? The pertinent switch was doubtless in plain sight and clearly marked, but again, he couldn't read the markings. As for his prisoners, they were being disturbingly quiet. In the back of his mind he had been anticipating some attempt to burn through the door—surely they had some sort of hand weapon back there which might serve the purpose—but they hadn't so much as pounded on it.

He hoped fervently that they were just being fatalistic about their captivity. If their silence meant that they were satisfied with it, that was bad news. The news was bad enough already, for he had no idea what he was going to do with them, or with the boat, when he got to Castle Wolfwhip—

And no time left to invent any plan, for in the next flash of lightning he saw the castle.

It was still several miles away, but even at this distance its massiveness was awe-inspiring. There were many towers in the city that were smaller; despite the lack of any adjacent structure with which to compare it, Chris guessed that the black, windowless pile could not be less than thirty stories high.

At first, he thought it was surrounded by a moat, but that was only an effect of foreshortening brought on by distance. Actually, it stood in the middle of a huge lake, so storm-lashed that Chris could not imagine how the clumsy swan boat could survive on it, let alone make any headway.

He pulled back on the throttles; but as he had suspected, the boat no longer answered to the manual controls. It plowed doggedly forward into the water. A moment later, the compressed air tanks blew with a bubbling roar, and the lake closed over the boat completely. It was now traveling on the bottom.

Now he no longer had even the lightning flashes to see by—nothing but the lights inside the boat, which did not penetrate the murky water at all. It was as though the transparent shell had abruptly gone opaque.

After what seemed a long while—though it was probably no more than ten minutes—the treads made a grinding noise, as if they had struck stone, and the vehicle came gradually to a halt. On a hunch, Chris tried the manuals again, but there was still no response.

Then the outside lights came on.

The swan boat was sitting snugly in a berth within a sizable cavern. Through the rills of yellow water draining down its sides, Chris saw that it had a reception committee: four men, with rifles. They looked down into the boat at him, grinning unpleasantly. While he stared helplessly back, the engines quit—

—and the outside door swung open.

They put him in the same cell with Anderson and Dulany. His guardian was appalled to see him—"Gods of all stars, Irish, now they're snatching children!"—and then, after he had heard the story, thoroughly disgusted. Dulany, as usual, said very little, but he did not look exactly pleased.

"There's probably a standard recognition signal you should have sent, except that you wouldn't have known what it was," Anderson said. "These petty barons did a lot of fighting among themselves before we got here—

fleecing us is probably the first project they've been together on since this mudball was colonized."

"Bluster," Dulany commented.

"Yes, it's part of the feudal *mores*. Chris, those men in the boat are going to take a lot of ribbing from their peers, regardless of the fact that they were never in any danger and they had sense enough to let you spin your own noose. They'll be likely to take it out on you when you're taken out for questioning."

"I've already been interviewed," Chris said grimly. "And they did."

"You have? Murder! There goes that one up the flue, Irish."

"Complication," Dulany agreed.

Anderson fell silent, leaving Chris to wonder what they had been talking about. Evidently they had been planning something which his news had torpedoed—though it was hard to imagine even the beginnings of such a plan, for their captors, out of a respect for the two Okies which Chris knew to be more than justified, had left them nothing but their underwear. At last the boy said hesitantly:

"What could I have done if my interview were still coming up?"

"Located our space suits," Anderson said gloomily. "Not that they'd have let you search the place, that's for sure, but you might have gotten a hint, or tricked them into dropping one. Even wary men sometimes underestimate youngsters. Now we'll just have to think of something else."

"There are dozens of space suits standing around the wall of that big audience chamber," Chris said. "If you could only get there, maybe one of them would fit one of you."

Dulany only smiled slightly. Anderson said: "Those aren't suits, Chris; they're armor—plate armor. Useless here, but they have some kind of heraldic significance; I think the barons used to collect them from each other, like scalps."

"That may be," Chris said stubbornly, "but there were at least two real suits there. I'm sure of that."

The two sergeants looked at each other. "Is it possible—?" Anderson said. "They've got the bravado for it, all right."

"Could be."

"By Sirius, there's a bluff we've got to call! Get busy on that lock, Irish!"

"In my underwear? Nix."

"What difference does that—oh, I see." Anderson grimaced impatiently. "We'll have to wait for lights out. Happily it won't be long."

"How are you going to bust the lock, Sergeant Dulany?" Chris asked. "It's almost as big as my head!"

"Those are the easy kinds," Dulany said loquaciously.

Chris in fact never did find out what Dulany did with the lock, for the operation was performed in the dark. Standing as instructed all the way to the back of the cell, he did not even hear anything until the huge, heavy door was thrown back with a thunderous crash.

The crash neatly drowned out the only yell the guard outside managed to get off. In this thunder-ridden fortress, nobody would think anything of such a noise. Then there was a jangle of keys, and two loud clicks as the unfortunate man was manacled with his own handcuffs. The Okies rolled him into the cell.

"What'll I do if he comes to?" Chris whispered hoarsely.

"Won't for hours," Dulany's voice said. "Shut the door. We'll be back."

From the boarding-squad sergeant, nine words all in one speech had the reassuring force of an oration. Chris grinned and shut the door.

Nothing seemed to happen thereafter for hours, ex-

89

cept that the thunder got louder. That was certainly no novelty on Heaven. But was it possible for even the heaviest thunderclap to shake a pile of stone as squat and massive as Castle Wolfwhip? Surely it couldn't last long if that were the case—and yet it was obviously at least a century old, probably more.

The fourth such blast answered his question. It was an explosion, and it was *inside* the building. In response, all the lights came on; and Chris saw that the door had been jarred open.

When he went over to close it again, he found himself looking down a small precipice. The corridor floor had collapsed. Several stunned figures were sitting amid the rubble it had made on the story below it. Considering the size of the blocks of which it had been made, they were lucky that it hadn't killed them.

Still another explosion, and this time the lights went back out. Quite evidently, the suits Chris had seen in the audience hall had indeed been Anderson's and Dulany's battle dress. Well, this ought to cure the baron of Castle Wolfwhip of the habit of exhibiting his scalps. It ought to cure him of the habit of kidnapping Okies, too. It occurred to Chris that the whole plan of using Anderson and Dulany as hostages, even in their underwear, was about as safe an operation as trying to imprison two demons in a corncrib.

Then they were back. Seeing them hovering in the collapsed corridor, their helmet lamps making a shifting, confusing pattern of shadows, Chris realized, too, what kind of vehicle the city would have sent out after him if he had managed to get word back.

"You all right?" Anderson's PA speaker demanded. "Good. Didn't occur to me that the floor might go."

They came into the cell. The guard, who had just recovered his senses, took one look and crawled into the corner farthest from the two steel figures.

"Now we've got a problem. We've got a safe-conduct

out of the castle, but we can't carry you through that storm, and we don't dare risk putting you in one of their suits."

"Boat," Dulany said, pointing at Chris.

"That's right, I forgot, he knows how to drive one. Okay, boy, stick your elbows out and we'll fly you out to where there's a floor you can walk on. Irish, let's go."

"One minute." Dulany unhooked a bunch of keys from his waist and tossed them into the corner where the guard was cowering. "Right."

Only Anderson joined him in the swan boat, still in his armor; Dulany stayed airborne, in radio communication with Anderson, in case the colonials should have the notion of making the boat turn around and return home on autopilot. After he saw the holes the two cops had torn through the great walls of Castle Wolfwhip, Chris doubted that they'd even entertain such a notion, but obviously it was sensible not to take chances where it wasn't necessary.

The moment the boat was crawling across the bottom of the lake, Anderson took his helmet off and turned promptly to studying the control board. Finally he nodded and snapped three switches.

"That should do it."

"Do what?"

"Prevent them from putting this tub under remote control. In fact from this point on they won't even be able to locate her. Now Irish can shoot on ahead of us and get the word to the Mayor." He put the helmet back on and spoke briefly, then doffed it.

"Now, Chris," he said grimly, "comes the riot act."

8

THE GHOSTS OF SPACE

The "riot act" was every bit as unpleasant as he had foreseen it would be, but somehow he managed to live through it—mostly by bearing in mind as firmly as possible that he had it coming. He was never likely to become a real Okie by stealing the property of people who had hired the city on to do a job, no matter how good he thought his reasons were.

And in this first disastrous instance he had simply been in the way. The city would have known soon enough in any event of the fact that Anderson and Dulany were being held prisoner, since the colonists of Heaven could not have used them effectively as hostages without notifying Amalfi of the fact; and there was no doubt in Chris's mind that the two cops could have gotten out of Castle Wolfwhip without his intervention, and perhaps a good deal faster, too. Above all, they might have been gotten out by Amalfi *without violence*, and thus saved the contract intact. The appearance of Chris as a third prisoner had been totally unwelcomed to *both* sides, and had turned what had been merely a tense situation into an explosion.

In the end, they gave him full marks for imagination and boldness, as well as for coolness under fire, but by that time Chris had learned enough about the situation to feel that his chances of ever becoming a citizen were not worth an Oc dollar. The new contract was considerably more limited than the old, and called for reparations for the damage the two sergeants had done to Castle Wolfwhip; under it, the city stood to gain considerably less than before.

Chris was astonished that there was any new contract at all, and said so, rather hesitantly. Anderson explained:

"Violence between employer and employee is as old as man, Chris, but the work has to be done all the same. The colonists as a corporate entity disown the kidnapper and claim the right to deal with him according to their own system of justice, which we're bound to respect. Damage to real property, on the other hand, has to be paid for—and the city can't disown Irish and me because we're officers and agents of the city."

"But what about the scheme to ground the city and take it over?"

"We know nothing about that except what you overheard. That would have no status in a colonial court, and probably wouldn't even if you were a citizen—in this case, if you were of legal age."

And there it was again. "Well, there's something else I've been wondering about," Chris said. "Why is the age to start the drugs fixed at eighteen? Wouldn't they work at any age? Suppose we took aboard a man forty years old who also happened to be a red-hot expert at something we needed. Couldn't you start him on the drugs anyhow?"

"We could and we would," Anderson assured him. "Eighteen is only the *optimum* age, the earliest age at which we can be sure the specimen is physically mature. You see the drugs can't set the clock back. They just arrest aging from the moment when they're first given. Tell me, have you ever heard of the legend of Tithonus?"

"No, I'm afraid not."

"I don't know it very well myself; ask the City Fathers.

But briefly, he got himself in the good books of the goddess of dawn, Eos, and asked for the gift of immortality. She gave it to him, but he was pretty old at the time. When he realized that he was just going to stay that way forever, he asked Eos to take the gift back. So she changed him into a grasshopper, and you know how long *they* live."

"Hmm. A man who was going to be a permanent seventy-five wouldn't be much good to himself, I guess. Or to the city either."

"That's the theory," the perimeter sergeant agreed. "But of course we have to take 'em as we find 'em. Amalfi went on the drugs at fifty—which, for him, happened to be his prime."

Thus his education went on, much as before, except that he stayed scrupulously away from the docks. Since the new contract was limited to three months, there probably wouldn't have been much to see down there anyhow—or so he told himself, not without a suspicion that there were a few holes in his logic. In addition, he got some sympathy and support from a wholly unexpected source: Piggy Kingston-Throop.

"It just goes to show you how much truth there is in all this jabber about citizenship," he said fiercely, at their usual after-class meeting. "Here you go and do them a big fat favor, and all they can think of to do is lecture you for getting in their way. They even go right on doing business with these guys who were going to grab the city if they could."

"Well, we do have to eat."

"Yeah, but it's dirty money all the same. Come to think of it, though, if I'd have been in your shoes I'd have handled it differently."

"I know," Chris said, "that's what they all keep telling me. I should never have gotten into the boat in the first place."

"Pooh, that part's all right," Piggy said scornfully. "If

you hadn't gotten into the boat they'd never have known about the plot to take the city—that's the favor you did them, and don't you forget it. They're on their guard now. No, I mean what happened after you locked the guys up in the back cabin. You said that the boat had bumped into the dock and was trying to climb it, right?"

"Yes."

"And a lot of cops came running?"

"I don't know about a lot," Chris said cautiously. "There were three or four, I think."

"Okay. Now if it had been me, I would have just stopped the boat right there, and gotten out, and told the cops what I'd heard. Let *them* drag it out of the guys you'd locked up. You know how the City Fathers cram all that junk into our heads in class—well, they can take stuff out the same way. Dad says it's darned unpleasant for the victim, but they get it."

Chris could only shrug helplessly. "You're right. That would have been the sensible thing to do. And it seems obvious the way you tell it. But all I can say is, it didn't occur to me." He thought a moment, and then added: "But in a way I'm not too sorry, Piggy. That way, I never would have gotten to Castle Wolfwhip at all— sure, it would have been better if I hadn't—but it sure was exciting while I was there."

"Boy, I'll bet it was! I wish I'd been there!" Piggy began to shadowbox awkwardly. "I wouldn't have hidden in any cell, believe you me. I'd have showed 'em!"

Chris did his best not to laugh. "Going by what I heard, if you'd gone along with the sergeants—if they'd let you—you'd have been killed by your own friends. Those weren't just rotten eggs they were throwing around."

"All the same, I'll bet—Hullo, we're lifting."

The city had not lifted yet, but Chris knew what Piggy meant; he too could hear the deepening hum of the spindizzies. "So we are. That three months sure went by in a hurry."

"Three months isn't much in space. We'll be eighteen before we know it."

"That," Chris said gloomily, "is exactly what I'm afraid of."

"Well, *I* don't give a darn. This whole deal about your running off with the boat proves that they don't mean what they say about earning citizenship. Like I say, the whole thing's just a scheme to keep kids in line, so they won't have to be watched so much. The minute you actually *do* something for the survival of the city, bingo! the roof falls on you. Never mind that, it was a good thing to do and shows you've got guts—you've caused them trouble, and that's what the system's supposed to prevent."

There was, Chris saw, something to be said for the theory, no matter how exaggerated Piggy's way of putting it was. In Chris's present state of discouragement, it would be a dangerously easy point of view to adopt.

"Well, Piggy, what I want to know is, what are you going to do if you're wrong? I mean, supposing the City Fathers decide not to make you a citizen, and it turns out that they can't be fixed? Then you'll be stuck with being a passenger for the rest of your life—and it'd only be a normal lifetime, too."

"Passengers aren't as helpless as they think," Piggy said darkly. "Some one of these days the Lost City is going to come back, and when that happens, all of a sudden the passengers are going to be top dog."

"The Lost City? I never heard of it."

"Of course you haven't. And the City Fathers won't ever tell you about it, either. But word gets around."

"Okay, don't be mysterious," Chris said. "What's it all about?"

Piggy's voice dropped to a hoarse whisper. "Do you

swear not to tell anybody else, except another passenger?"

"Sure."

Piggy looked elaborately over both shoulders before going on. As usual, they were the only youngsters on the street, and none of the adults were paying the slightest attention to them.

"Well," he said in the same tone of voice, "it's like this. One of the first cities ever to take off was a big one. Nobody knows its name, but *I* think it was Los Angeles. Anyhow, it got lost, and ran out of drugs, and then out of food, way off in some part of space that was never colonized, so it couldn't find any work either. But then they made a planetfall on a new world, something nobody had ever seen before. It was like Earth—bigger, but the same gravity, and a little more oxygen in the air, and a perfect climate—like spring all year round, even at the poles. If you planted seeds there, you had to jump back in a hurry or the plant would hit you under the chin, they grew so fast.

"But that wasn't the half of it."

"It sounds like plenty," Chris said.

"That was all good, but they found something else even better. There was a kind of grain growing wild there, and when they analyzed it to see whether or not it was good to eat, *they found it contained an antideath drug*—not any of ours, but better than all of ours rolled into one. They didn't even have to extract it—all they had to do was make bread out of the plant."

"Wow. Piggy, is this just a story?"

"Well, I can't give you an affidavit," Piggy said, offended. "Do you want to hear the rest or don't you?"

"Go ahead," Chris said hastily.

"So then the question was, what were they going to do with their city? They didn't need it. Everything they needed came right up out of the ground while their backs were turned. So they decided to stock it up and send it out into space again, to look for other cities. Whenever they make contact with a new Okie town, they take all the passengers off—nobody else—and take them back to this planet where *everybody* can have the drugs, because there's never any shortage."

"Suppose the other city doesn't want to give up its passengers?"

"Why wouldn't it want to? If it had any use for them, they'd be citizens, wouldn't they?"

"Yes, but just suppose."

"They'd give them up anyhow. Like I said, the Lost City is *big*."

Unfortunately for the half-million other questions Chris wanted to ask, at that point the city moaned softly to the sound of the take-cover siren. The boys parted hurriedly; but Chris, after a moment's thought, did not go home. Instead, he holed up in a public information booth, where he fed his card into the slot and asked for the Librarian.

He had promised not to mention the Lost City to anyone but another passenger, which ruled out questioning his guardian, or the City Fathers directly; but he had thought of a way to ask an indirect question. The Librarian was that one of the 134 machines comprising the City Fathers which had prime charge of the memory banks, and was additionally charged with teaching; it did not collect information, but only catalogued and dispensed it. Interpretation was not one of its functions.

"CARD ACCEPTED. PROCEED."

"Question: Do any antiagathics grow naturally—I mean, do they occur in plants that could be raised as crops?"

A brief pause. "A PRECURSOR OF THE ANTISLEEP DRUG IS A STEROID SUBSTANCE OCCURRING NATURALLY IN A NUMBER OF YAMLIKE PLANTS FOUND ON EARTH, LARGELY IN CENTRAL AND SOUTH AMERICA. THIS SAPOGENIN IS NOT, HOWEVER, IN ITSELF AN ANTIAGATHIC, AND MUST BE CON-

VERTED; HUNDREDS OF DIFFERENT STEROIDS ARE PRODUCED FROM THE SAME STARTING MATERIAL.

"ASCOMYCIN IS PRODUCED BY DEEP-TANK FERMENTATION OF A MICROORGANISM AND HARVESTED FROM THE BEER. THIS PROCEDURE MIGHT BROADLY BE DEFINED AS CROP-RAISING.

"ALL OTHER KNOWN ANTIAGATHICS ARE WHOLLY SYNTHETIC DRUGS."

Chris sat back, scratching his head in exasperation. He had hoped for a clear-cut, yes-or-no answer, but what he had gotten stood squarely in the middle. No antiagathics were harvested from real crops; but if a crop plant could produce something at least enough like an antiagathic to be converted into one, then that part of Piggy's astounding story was at least possible. Unhappily, he could think of no further questions sufficiently indirect to keep his main point of interest hidden.

Then he noticed that the booth had not returned his card to him. This was quite usual; it meant only that the Librarian, which spent its whole mechanical life substituting free association for thinking, had a related subject it would talk about if he liked. Usually it wasn't worth while exploring these, for the Librarian could go on forever if so encouraged; all he needed to do now was to say "Return," and he could take his card and go. But the take-cover alert wasn't over yet; so, instead, he said, "Proceed."

"SUBJECT, ANTIAGATHICS AS BY-PRODUCTS OF AGRICULTURE. SUB-SUBJECT, LEGENDARY IDYLLIC PLANETS." Chris sat bolt upright. "ANTIAGATHICS AS BY-PRODUCTS OF AGRICULTURE, USUALLY IN THE DAILY BREAD, IS ONE OF THE COMMON FEATURES OR DIAGNOSTIC SIGNS OF THE LEGENDARY PLANETS OF NOMAD-CITY MYTHOLOGY. OTHERS INCLUDE: EARTHLIKE GRAVITY BUT GREATER LAND AREA; EARTHLIKE ATMOSPHERE BUT MORE ABUNDANT OXYGEN; EARTHLIKE WEATHER BUT WITH UNIFORM CLIMATE, AND COMPLETE ISOLATION FROM EXISTING TRADE LANES. NO PLANET

MATCHING THIS DESCRIPTION IN ANY PARTICULAR HAS YET BEEN FOUND. NAMES OFTEN GIVEN TO SUCH WORLDS IN- CLUDE: ARCADY, BRADBURY, CELEPHAIS . . ."

Chris was so stunned that the Librarian had worked its way all the way through "ZIMIAMVIA" and had begun another alphabetical catalogue before he thought to ask for his card back. His question had not been very crafty, after all.

By the time he emerged from the booth, the storms of Heaven had vanished and the city was once more soar- ing amid the stars. Furthermore, he was late for dinner.

So, after all, there had been no secret to keep. Chris told the Andersons the story of his failure to outwit the Librarian; it made the best possible excuse for his late- ness, since it was true, and it reduced Carla to tears of helpless laughter. The perimeter sergeant was amused, too, but there was an undercurrent of seriousness be- neath his amusement.

"You're learning, Chris. It's easy to think that because the City Fathers are dead, they're also stupid; but you see that that isn't the case. Otherwise they would never have been given the power that they wield—and in some departments their power is absolute."

"Even over the Mayor?"

"Yes and no. They can't forbid the Mayor anything. But if he goes against their judgment more often than they're set to tolerate, they can revoke his office. That's never happened here, but if it does, we'll have to sit still for it. If we don't, they'll stop the machinery.

"Wow. Isn't it dangerous to give machines so much power? Suppose they had a breakdown?"

"If there were only a few of them, that would be a real danger; but there are more than a hundred, and they monitor and repair each other, so in fact it will never happen. Sanity and logic is their stock in trade— which is why they can accept or reject the results of any election we may run. The popular will is sometimes an idiot, but no human being can be given the power to overrule it; not safely. But the machines can.

"Of course, there are stories about towns whose City Fathers ran amok with them. They're just stories, like Piggy's 'Lost City'—but they're important even when they're not true. Whenever a new way of living appears in the universe, the people who adopt it see quickly enough that it isn't perfect. They try to make it better, sure; but there are always some things about it that can't be changed. And the hopes and fears that are centered on those points get turned into stories.

"Piggy's myth, for instance. We live long lives in the cities, but not everybody can have the gift. It's impossible that everyone should have it—the whole universe isn't big enough to contain the sheer mass of flesh that would accumulate if we all lived and bred as long as we each wanted to. Piggy's myth says it is possible, which is untrue; but what *is* true about it is that it points to one of the real dissatisfactions with our way of living, real because nothing can be done about it.

"The story of the runaway City Fathers is another. No such thing has ever happened as far as I know, and it doesn't seem to be possible. But no live man *likes* to take orders from a bunch of machines, or to think that he may lose his life if they say so—but he might, because the City Fathers are the jury aboard most cities. So he invents a cautionary tale about City Fathers running amok, though actually he's talking not about the machines at all—he's warning that *he* may run amok if he's pushed too far.

"The universe of the cities is full of these ghosts. Sooner or later somebody is going to tell you that some cities go bindlestiff."

"Somebody has," Chris admitted. "But I didn't know what he meant."

"It's an old Earth term. A hobo was an honest migratory worker, who lived that way because he liked it. A tramp was the same kind of fellow, except that he wouldn't work—he lived by stealing or begging from settled people. In hobo society both kinds were more or less respectable. But the bindlestiff was a migrant who stole from other migrants—he robbed their bindles, the bags they carried their few belongings in. That man was an outcast from both worlds.

"It's common talk that some cities in trouble have gone bindlestiff—taken to preying on other cities. Again, there are no specific instances. IMT is the town that's most often mentioned, but the last we heard of IMT, she wasn't a bindlestiff—she'd been outlawed for a horrible crime on a colony planet, but technically that makes her only a tramp. A mean one, but still only a tramp."

"I see," Chris said slowly. "It's like the story about City Fathers going crazy. Cities do starve, I know that; and the bindlestiff story says, 'How will *we* behave when the pinch comes?' "

Anderson looked gratified. "Look at that," he said to Carla. "Maybe I should have been a teacher!"

"Nothing to do with you," Carla said composedly. "Chris is doing all the thinking. Besides, I like you better as a cop."

The perimeter sergeant sighed, a little ruefully. "Oh, well, all right. Then I'll give you only one more story. You've heard of the Vegan orbital fort?"

"Oh, sure. That was in the history, way back."

"Good. Well, for once, that's a real thing. There was a Vegan orbital fort, and it did get away, and nobody knows where it is now. The City Fathers say that it probably died when it ran out of supplies, but it was a pretty big job and might well have survived under circumstances no ordinary city could live through. If you ask the City Fathers for the probabilities, they tell you that they can't give you any figures—which is a bad sign in itself.

"Now, that's as far as the facts go. But there's a legend to go with them. The legend says that the fort is foraging through the trade lanes, devouring cities—just the way a dragonfly catches mosquitoes, on the wing. Nobody has actually seen the fort since the scorching of Vega, but the legend persists; every time a city disappears, the word goes around, first, that a bindlestiff got it, and next, that the fort got it.

"What's it all about, Chris? Tell me."

Chris thought for a long time. At last he said:

"I'm kind of confused. It ought to be the same kind of story as the others—something people are afraid of. Like meeting up some day with a planet, like the Vegan system, where the people have more on the ball than we do and will gobble us up the way we did Vega—"

Anderson's big fist crashed down on the dinner table, making all the plates jump. "Precisely!" he crowed. "Look there, Carla—"

Carla's own hands reached out and covered the sergeant's fist gently. "Dear, Chris isn't through yet. You didn't give him a chance to finish."

"I didn't? But—sorry, Chris. Go ahead."

"I don't know whether I'm through or not," Chris said, embarrassed and floundering. "This one story just confuses me. It's not as simple as the others; I think I'm sure of that."

"Go ahead."

"Well, it's sensible to be afraid of meeting somebody stronger than yourself. It might well happen. And there is a real Vegan orbital fort, or at least there was one. The other stories don't have that much going for them that's real—except the things people are actually afraid of, the things the stories *actually* are about. Does this make sense?"

"Yes. The things the stories symbolize."

"That's the word. To be afraid of the fort is to be afraid of a real thing. But what does the story symbolize? It's got to be the same kind of thing in the end—the fear people have of themselves. The story says, 'I'm tired of working to be a citizen, and obeying the Earth cops, and protecting the city, and living a thousand years with machines bossing me, and taking sass from colonists, and I don't know what all else. If I had a great big city that I could run all by myself, I'd spend the next thousand years smashing things up!'"

There was a long, long silence, during which Chris became more and more convinced that he had again talked out of turn, and far too much. Carla did not seem to be upset, but her husband looked stunned and wrathful.

"There *is* something wrong with the apprenticeship system," he growled at last, though he did not appear to be speaking to either of them. "First the Kingston-Throop kid—and now this. Carla! You're the brains in the family. Did it ever occur to you that that fort legend had anything to do with education?"

"Yes, dear. Long ago."

"Why didn't you say so?"

"I would have said so as soon as we had a child; until then, it wasn't any of my business. Now Chris has said it for me."

The perimeter sergeant turned a lowering face on Chris. "You," he said, "are a holy terror. I set out to teach you, as I was charged to do, and you wind up teaching me. Not even Amalfi knows this side of the fort story, I'll swear to that—and when he hears it, there's going to be a real upheaval in the schools."

"I'm sorry," Chris said miserably. He did not know what else to say.

"Don't be sorry!" Anderson roared, surging to his feet. "Stick to your guns! Let the other guy be afraid of ghosts—you know the one thing about ghosts that

104

you need to know, no matter what kind of ghosts they are: They have nothing to do with the dead. It's *always* themselves that people are afraid of."

He looked about distractedly. "I've got to go topside. Here's my hurry—where's my hat?" He roared out, banging one hand against the side of the door, leaving Chris frozen with alarm.

Then Carla began to laugh all over again.

9

THE TRAMP

But if the errand on behalf of which Sgt. Anderson had undertaken his rhinoceros-charge exit had really had anything to do with education, Chris had yet to see it reflected in his own. That got steadily harder, as the City Fathers, blindly and impersonally assuming that he had comprehended what they had already stuffed into his head, began to build his store of knowledge toward some threshold where it would start to be useful for the survival of the city. As this process went forward, Chris's old headaches dwindled into the category of passing twinges; these days, he sometimes felt actively, physically sick from sheer inability to make sense of what was being thrust upon him. In a moment of revulsion, he told the City Fathers so.

"It will pass. The normal human being feels an average of twenty small pains per hour. If any persist, report to Medical."

No, he was not going to do that; he was not going to be invalided out of his citizenship if he could help it. Yet it seemed to him that what he was suffering couldn't fairly be called "small pains." What to do, since he feared that Medical's cure would be worse than the disease? He didn't want to worry the Andersons, either —he had repaid their kindnesses with enough trouble already.

That left nobody to talk to but Dr. Braziller, that fearsome old harpy who seldom spoke in any language but logarithms and symbolic logic. Chris stood off from this next-but-worst choice for weeks; but in the end he had to do it. Though there was nothing physically wrong with him even now, he had the crazy notion that the City Fathers were about to kill him; one more stone of fact on his head and his neck would break.

"And well it might," Dr. Braziller told him, in her office after class. "Chris, the City Fathers are not interested in your welfare; I suppose you know that. They're interested in only one thing: the survival of the city. That's their prime directive. Otherwise they have no interest in people at all; after all, they're only machines."

"All right," Chris said, blotting his brow with a trembling hand. "But Dr. Braziller, what good will it do the city for them to blow all my fuses? I've been trying, really I have. But it isn't good enough for them. They keep right on piling the stuff in, and it makes no *sense* to me!"

"Yes, I've noticed that. But there's reason behind what they're doing, Chris. You're almost eighteen; and they're probing for some entrance point into your talents—some spark that will take fire, some bent of yours that might some day turn into a valuable specialty."

"I don't think I have any," Chris said dully.

"Maybe not. That remains to be seen. If you have one, they'll find it; the City Fathers never miss on this kind of thing. But Chris, my dear, you can't expect it to be easy on you. Real knowledge is always hard to come by—and now that the machines think you might actually be of some use to the city—"

"But they can't think that! They haven't found anything!"

"I can't read their minds, because they haven't any," Dr. Braziller said quietly. "But I've seen them do this before. They wouldn't be driving you in this way if they didn't suspect that you're good for something. They're trying to find out what it is, and unless you want to give up right now, you're going to have to sit still while they look. It doesn't surprise me that it makes you ill. It made me ill, too; I feel a little queasy just remembering it, and that was eighty years ago."

She fell silent suddenly, and in that moment, she looked even older than she had ever seemed before . . . old, and frail, and deeply sad, and—could it be possible?—beautiful.

"Now and then I wonder if they were right," Dr. Braziller told the heaped papers on her desk. "I wanted to be a composer. But the City Fathers had never heard of a successful woman composer, and it's hard to argue with that kind of charge. No, Chris, once the machines have fingered you, you have to be what they want you to be; the only alternative is to be a passenger—which means, to be nothing at all. I don't wonder that it makes you ill. But, Chris—fight back, fight back! Don't let those cabinet-heads lick you! Stick them out. They're only probing, and the minute we find out what they want, we can bear down on it. I'll help wherever I can— *I hate those things*. But first, we have to find out what they want. Have you got the guts, Chris?"

"I don't know. I'll try. But I don't know."

"Nobody knows, yet. They don't know themselves— that's your only hope. They want to know what you can do. You have to show them. As soon as they find out, you will be a citizen—but until then, it's going to be rough, and there will be nothing that anybody can do to help you. It will be up to you, and you alone."

It was heartening to have another ally, but Chris would have found Dr. Braziller's whole case more convincing had he been able to see the faintest sign of a talent—any talent at all—emerging under the ungentle ministrations of the machines. True, lately they had been bearing down heavily on his interest in history—but what good was that aboard an Okie city? The City Fathers themselves were the city's historians, just as they were its library, its accounting department, its schools and much of its government. No live person was needed to teach the subject or to write about it, and at best, as far as Chris could see, it could never be more than a hobby for an Okie citizen.

Even in the present instance, Chris was not being called upon to *do* anything with history put pass almost incredibly hard tests in it—tests which consisted largely of showing that he had retained all of the vast mass of facts that the City Fathers were determinedly shoving into him. And this was no longer just history from the Okie point of view. Whole systems of world and interstellar history—Machiavelli, Plutarch, Thucydides, Gibbon, Marx, Pareto, Spengler, Sarton, Toynbee, Durant and a score of others—came marching through the gray gas into his head, without mercy and with apparent indifference to the fact that they all contradicted each other fatally at crucial points.

There was no punishment for failures, since the City Fathers' pedagogy made failure of memory impossible, and it was only his memory that they seemed to be exploiting here. Instead, punishment was continuous: It lay in the certainty that though today's dose had been fiendish, tomorrow's would be worse.

"Now there you're wrong," Dr. Braziller told him. "Dead though they are, the machines aren't ignorant of human psychology—far from it. They know very well that some students respond better to reward than to punishment, and that others have to be driven by fear. The second kind is usually the less intelligent, and they know that too; how could they *not* know it after so many generations of experience? You're lucky that they've put you in the first category."

"You mean they're *rewarding* me?" Chris squeaked indignantly.

"Certainly."

"But how?"

"By letting you go on studying even when they're not satisfied with your progress. That's quite a concession, Chris."

"Maybe so," Chris said glumly. "But I'd get the point faster if they handed out lollipops instead."

Dr. Braziller had never heard of lollipops; she was an Okie. She only responded, a little primly: "You'd get it fast enough if they decided on a punishment system for you instead. They're rigidly just, but know nothing about mercy; and leniency with children is utterly foreign to them—which is one reason why I'm here."

The city hummed onward, and so did the days—and the months. Only Chris seemed to be making no progress in any visible direction.

No, that wasn't quite true. Piggy was going nowhere, either, as far as Chris could see. But there the situation was even more puzzling and full of complications. To begin with, ever since Chris had first met him, Piggy had been denying that he cared about what happened to him when he turned eighteen; so it was odd—though not entirely surprising—to discover that he did care, after all. In fact, though his situation appeared to be now quite hopeless, Piggy was full of loud self-confidence, belied in the next breath by dark hints of mysterious plans to cinch what was supposed to be cinched already, and even darker hints of awful things to come if it didn't turn out to be cinched. It was all more than Chris could manage to sort out, especially considering his inability to see more than half a minute into his own future. Some days he felt as though Piggy's old accusation—"Boy, you *are* dumb!"—were written on his forehead in letters of fire.

Although Piggy said almost nothing about it, Chris gathered that he had already approached his father on the subject of biasing the City Fathers in his favor on the Citizenship Tests, and had been rebuffed with a loud roar, only slightly tempered by the intervention of his mother. There was of course no way to study for the Tests, since they measured nothing but potentials, not achievements; which meant, in turn, that there was no such thing as a pony or a crib for them.

Now, it was obvious, Piggy was thinking back to Chris's adventure on Heaven. Judging by the questions he asked about it, Chris deduced that Piggy was searching for something heroic to do, in order to do it much better than Chris had. Chris was human enough to doubt that Piggy could make a much better showing, but in any event the city was still in space, so no opportunity offered itself.

Occasionally, too, he would disappear after class for several days running. On his return, his story was that he had been prowling around the city eavesdropping on the adult passengers. They were, Piggy said, up to something—just possibly, the building of a secret Dirac transmitter with which to call the Lost City. Chris did not believe a word of this, nor did he think Piggy did either.

The simple, granite-keel facts were that time was running out for both of them, and that desperation was setting in: for Piggy because he had never tried, and for Chris because nothing he tried seemed to get him anywhere. All around them their younger schoolmates seemed to be opening into talents with the violence and unpredictability of popcorn, turning everything the memory cells fed them into salt and savor no matter how high the heat was turned up. In comparison, Chris felt as retarded as a dinosaur, and just as clumsy and gigantic.

It was in this atmosphere of pervasive, incipient failure that Sgt. Anderson one evening said calmly:

"Chris, the Mayor wants to talk to you."

From anyone else, Chris would have taken such an announcement as a practical joke, too absurd to be even upsetting. From Sgt. Anderson he did not know how to take it; he simply stared.

"Relax—it isn't going to be an ordeal, and besides I didn't say he wanted to *see* you. Sit back down and I'll explain."

Numbly, Chris did so.

"What's happened is this: We're approaching another job of work. From the first contacts we had with these people, it sounded simple and straightforward, but of course nothing ever is. (Amalfi says the biggest lie it's possible to tell in the English language is, 'It was as simple as that.') Supposedly we were going to be hired on to do a straightforward piece of local geology and mining—nothing so tricky as changing the whole setup of a planet, just a standard piece of work. You've seen the motto on City Hall?"

Chris had. It read: Mow YOUR LAWN, LADY? It had never seemed very dignified to him, but he was beginning to understand what it implied. He nodded.

"Well, that's the way it's always supposed to be: We come in, we do a job, we go out again. Local feuds don't count; we take no part in them.

"But as we got closer to signing a contract with this place—it's called Argus Three—we began to get hints that we were second comers. Apparently there'd already been one city on Argus, hired to do the job, but hadn't done it well.

"We tried to find out more about this, naturally, to be sure the Argidae were telling a straight story; we didn't want to be poaching on any other city's contract. But the colonists were very vague about the whole thing. Finally, though, they let it slip that the other city was still sitting on their planet, and still claimed to be working on the job, even though the contract deadline

112

had passed. Tell me—what would you do in a case like that, if you were Amalfi?"

Chris frowned. "I don't know any other answer but the one in the books. If the planet has an overstayed city, it's supposed to call the cops. All other cities should stay clear, otherwise they might get involved in the shooting, if there is any."

"Right; and this appears to be a classic case. The colonists can't be too explicit because they know that every word they broadcast to us is going to be overheard; but the City Fathers have analyzed what Argus Three *has* sent us, and the chances are a hundred to one that that other city has settled on Argus Three for good . . . in short, that it means to take over the planet. The Argidae don't want to call the cops, for reasons we don't know. Instead, they seem to be trying to hire us to take on this tramp city and clear him out. If we tackle that, there *will* be shooting, that's for sure—and the cops will probably show up anyhow before it's over.

"Obviously, as you say, the thing to do is get out of the vicinity, fast. Cities ought not to fight with each other, let alone get involved in anything like a Violation. But Argus Three's offering us sixty-three million dollars in metal to slough them of the tramp before the cops arrive, and the Mayor thinks we can do it. Also, he hates tramps—I think he might even have taken on the job for nothing. The fact, anyhow, is that he *has* taken it."

The perimeter sergeant paused and eyed Chris, seemingly waiting for comments. At last Chris said: "What did the City Fathers say?"

"They said NO in a loud voice until the money was mentioned. After that they ran an accounting of the treasury, and gave Amalfi his head. They had a few additional facts to work from that I haven't told you yet, most of which seem to indicate that we can dispossess this tramp without too much damage to our own

113

city, and very possibly before the cops even hear that anything's happening. All the same, bear in mind that they think of nothing but the city as a whole. If some of us get killed in the process they won't care, as long as the city itself gets off cleanly. They're not sentimental."

"I already know that," Chris said, with feeling. "But— how do I come into all this? Why does the Mayor want to talk to me? I don't know anything but what you've told me—and besides, he's already made up his mind."

"He's made up his mind," Anderson agreed, "but you know a lot that he doesn't know. As we get closer to Argus Three, he wants you to listen to the broadcasts from the Argidae, and anything we may pick up from the tramp, and fill him in on any clues you hear."

"But why?"

"Because you're the only person on board who knows the tramp at first hand," the perimeter sergeant said, with slow, deliberate emphasis. "It's your old friend Scranton."

"But—that can't be so! There were hundreds of us put on board from Scranton—all adults but me—"

"Press-gang sweepings," Anderson said with cold disgust. "Oh, there were one or two specialists we found a use for, but none of them ever paid any attention to city politics. The rest were bulgy-muscled misfits, a large proportion of them psychotics. We cured them, but we couldn't raise their IQ's; without something to sell, or the Interplanetary Grand Prix, or heavy labor to keep their minds off their minds, they're just so many vegetables. We—Irish and I—couldn't find even one worth taking into our squads. We've made citizens of the three good specialists, but the rest will be passengers till they die.

"But you're the happy accident of that crew right now, Chris. The City Fathers say that your history aboard Scranton shows that you *know* something about the town. Amalfi wants to mine that knowledge. Want to tackle it?"

114

"I—I'll try."

"Good." The perimeter sergeant turned to the miniature tape recorder at his elbow. "Here's a complete transcript of everything we've heard from Argus Three so far. After you've heard it and made any comments that occur to you, Amalfi will begin to feed us the live messages, from the bridge. Ready?"

"No," Chris said, more desperately than he could ever have imagined possible for him. "Not yet. My head is about to bust already. Do I get off from school while this is going on? I couldn't take it, otherwise."

"No," Anderson said, "you don't. If a live message comes through while you're in class, we'll pull you out. But you'll go right back in again. Otherwise your schooling will go right on just as before, and if you can't take the new burden, well, that'll be too bad. You'd better get that straight right away, Chris. This isn't a vacation, and it isn't a prize. It's a job, *for the survival of the city*. Either you take it or you don't; either way, you get no special treatment. Well?"

For what seemed to him to be a long time, Chris sat and listened to his echoing Okie headache. At last, however, he said resignedly:

"I'll take it."

Anderson snapped the switch, and the tape began to run on the spools.

The earliest messages, as Anderson had noted, were vague and brief. The later ones were longer, but even more cryptic. Chris was able to worry very little more information out of them than Amalfi and the City Fathers already had. As promised, he spoke to Amalfi—but from the Andersons' apartment, through a hookup which fed what he had to say to the mayor and to the machines simultaneously.

The machines asked questions about population, energy resources, degree of automation and other vital matters, not a one of which Chris could answer. The Mayor mostly just listened; on the few occasions when his heavy voice cut in, Chris was unable to figure out what he was getting at.

"Chris, this railroad you mentioned; how long before you were born had it been pulled up?"

"About a century, sir, I think. You know Earth went back to the railroads in the middle two thousands, when all the fossil fuels ran out and they had to give up the highways to farmland."

"No, I didn't know that. All right, go ahead."

Now the City Fathers were asking him about armament. He had no answer for that one, either.

There came a day, however, when this pattern changed suddenly and completely. He was, indeed, pulled out of class for the purpose, and hurried into a small anteroom containing little but a chair and two television screens. One of the screens showed Sgt. Anderson; the other, nothing but a testing pattern.

"Hello, Chris. Sit down and pay attention; this is important. We're getting a transmission from the tramp city. We don't know whether it's just a beacon or whether they want to talk to us. Amalfi thinks it's unlikely that they'd be putting out a beacon in their situation, regardless of the law—they've broken too many others already. He's going to try to raise them, now that you're here; he wants you to listen."

"Right, sir."

Chris could not hear his own city calling; but after only a few minutes—for they were quite close to Argus Three now—the test pattern on the other screen vanished, and Chris saw an odiously familiar face.

"Hullo. This here's Argus Three."

"'This here' is *not* Argus Three," Amalfi's deep voice said promptly. "'This here' is the city of Scranton, Penn-

116

sylvania, and there's no point in your hiding it. Get me your boss."

"Now wait a minute. Just who do you think—"

"This *here* is New York, New York, calling, and I said, 'Get me your boss.' Go do it."

The face by now was both sullen and confused. After a moment's hesitation, it vanished. The screen flickered, the test pattern came back briefly, and then a second familiar face was looking directly at Chris. It was impossible to believe that the man couldn't see him, and the idea was outright frightening.

"Hello, New York," he said, affably enough. "So you've got us figured out. Well, we've got you figured out, too. This planet is under contract to us; be notified."

"Recorded," Amalfi said. "We also have it a matter of record that you are in Violation. Argus Three has made a new contract with us. It'd be the wisest course to clear ground and spin."

The man's eyes did not waver. Chris realized suddenly that it was an image of Amalfi he was staring at, not at Chris himself. "Spin yourself," he said evenly. "Our argument is with the colonists, not with you. We don't spin without a Vacate order from the cops. Once you mix into this, you may find it hard to mix out again. Be notified."

"Your self-confidence," Amalfi said, "is misplaced. Recorded."

The image from Scranton contracted to a bright point and vanished. The Mayor said at once:

"Chris, do you know either of those guys?"

"Both of them, sir. The first one's a small-time thug named Barney. I think he was the one who killed my brother's dog when I was impressed, but I didn't see who did it."

"I know the type. Go ahead."

"The other one is Frank Lutz. He was the city manager when I was aboard. It looks as if he still is."

"What's a city manager? Never mind, I'll ask the machines. All right. He looks dangerous; is he?"

"Yes, sir, he is. He's smart and he's tricky—and he has no more feeling than a snake."

"Sociopath," Amalfi said. "Thought so. One more question: Does he know you?"

Chris thought hard before answering. Lutz had seen him only once, and had never had to think about him as an individual again—thanks to the lifesaving intervention of Frad Haskins. "Sir, he just might, but I'd say not."

"Okay. Give the details to the City Fathers and let them calculate the probabilities. Meanwhile we'll take no chances. Thanks, Chris. Joel, come topside, will you?"

"Yes, sir." Anderson waited until he heard the Mayor's circuit cut out. Then his image, too, seemed to be staring directly at Chris. In fact, it was.

"Chris, did you understand what Amalfi meant about taking no chances?"

"Uh—no, not exactly."

"He meant that we're to keep you out of this Lutz's sight. In other words, *no deFord expeditions on this job*. Is that clear?"

It was all too clear.

118

10

ARGUS ASLEEP

The Argus system was well named: It was not far inside a crowded and beautiful cluster of relatively young stars, so that the nights on its planet had indeed a hundred eyes, like the Argus of the myth. The youth of the cluster went far toward explaining the presence of Scranton, for like all third-generation stars, the sun of Argus was very rich in metals, and so were its planets.

Of these there were only a few—just seven, to be exact, of which only the three habitable ones had been given numbers, and only Argus III actually colonized; II was suitable only for Arabs, and IV for Eskimos. The other four planets were technically of the gas giant class, but they were rather undernourished giants; the largest of them was about the size of Sol's Neptune. The closeness of the stars in the cluster to each other had swept up much of the primordial gas before planet formation had gotten a good start; the Argus system was in fact the largest yet to be encountered in the cluster.

Argus III, as the city droned down over it, looked heart-stoppingly like Pennsylvania; Chris began to feel a little sorry for the coming dispossession of Scranton—of which he had no doubts whatsoever—for surely the planet must have provided an intolerable temptation. It was mountainous over most of its land area, which was considerable; water was confined to many thousands of lakes, and a few small and intensely salty seas. It was also heavily wooded—almost entirely with conifers, or plants much like them, for evolution here had not yet gotten as far as a flowering plant. The firlike trees had thick boles and reared up hundreds of feet, noble monsters with their many shoulders hunched, as they had to be to bear their own weight in the two-G gravitation of this metal-heavy planet. The first sound Chris heard on Argus III after the city grounded was the explosion of a nearby seed cone, as loud as a crack of thunder. One of the seeds broke a window on the thirtieth floor of the McGraw-Hill Greenhouse, and the startled staff there had had to hack it to bits with fire axes to stop its germinating on the rug.

Under these circumstances it hardly mattered where the city settled; there was iron everywhere; and conversely there was no place on the planet which would be out of eavesdropping or of missile range of Scranton, to the mutual inconvenience of both parties. Nevertheless, Amalfi chose a site with great care, one just over the horizon from the great scar in the ground Scranton had made during its fumbled mining attempt, and with the highest points of an Allegheny-like range reared up between the two Okies. Only then did the machinery begin to rumble out into the forests.

Chris was beginning to practice thinking like Amalfi—not very confidently to be sure, since he had never seen the man, but at least it made a good game. The landing, Chris concluded tentatively, had been chosen mostly to prevent Scranton from seeing what the city was doing without sending over planes; and secondly to prevent foot traffic between the two cities. Probably it would never come to warfare between the two cities, anyhow, for nothing would be more likely to bring the cops to the scene in a hurry; and besides, it was already quite clear from New York's history that Amalfi actively hated anything that did the city damage, whether it was bombs or only rust.

In the past, his most usual strategy had been to outsit the enemy. If that failed, he tried to outperform them. As a last resort, he tried to bring them into conflct with themselves. There were no pure cases of any of these policies on record—every example was a mixture, and a complicated one—but these three flavorings were the strongest, and usually one was far more powerful than the other two. When Amalfi salted his dish, you could hardly taste the pepper or the mustard.

Not everyone could eat it thereafter, either; there were, Chris suspected, more subtle schools of Okie cookery. But that was how Amalfi did it, and he was the only chef the city had. Thus far, the city had survived him, which was the only test that counted with the citizens and the City Fathers.

On Argus III, it seemed, Amalfi's hope was to starve Scranton out by outperforming it. The city had the contract; Scranton had lost it. The city could do the job; Scranton had made a mess of it, and left behind a huge yellow scar around its planetfall which might not heal for a century. And while New York worked and Scranton starved—here was where a faint pinch of outsittery was added to the broth—Scranton couldn't carry through on its desperate hope of seizing Argus III as a new home planet; though the Argidae could not yell for the cops at the first sign—or the last—of such a piracy, New York could, and would. Okie solidarity was strong, and included a firm hatred of the cops . . . but it did not extend to encouraging another incident like Thor V, or bucking the cops against another city like IMT. Even the outlaw must protect himself against the criminally insane, especially if they seem to be on his side.

Okay; if that was what Amalfi planned, so be it. There was nothing that Chris could say about it, anyhow. Amalfi was the mayor, and he had the citizens and the

City Fathers behind him. Chris was only a youngster and a passenger.

But he knew one thing about the plan that neither Amalfi nor any other New Yorker could know, except himself:

It was not going to work.

He knew Scranton; the city didn't. If this was how Amalfi planned to proceed against Frank Lutz, it would fail.

But was he reading Amalfi's mind aright? That was probably the first question. After several days of worrying—which worsened his school record drastically—he took the question to the only person he knew who had ever seen Amalfi: his guardian.

"I can't tell you what Amalfi's set us up to do, you aren't authorized to know," the perimeter sergeant said gently. "But you've done a lot of good guessing. As far as you've guessed, Chris, you're pretty close."

Carla banged a coffee cup angrily into a saucer. "Pretty close? Joel, all this male expertise is a pain in the neck. Chris is right and you know it. Give him a break and tell him so."

"I'm not authorized," Anderson said doggedly, but from him that was tantamount to an admission. "Besides, Chris is wrong on one point. We can't sit here forever, just to prevent this tramp from taking over Argus Three. Sooner or later we'll have to be on our own way, and we can't overstay our contract, either—we've got Violations of our own on our docket that we care about, whether Scranton cares about Violations or not. We have a closing date that we mean to observe—and that makes the problem *much* stiffer."

"I see it does," Chris said diffidently. "But at least I understood part of it. And it seems to me that there are two big holes in it—and I just hope I'm wrong about those."

"Holes?" the perimeter sergeant said. "Where? What are they?"

"Well, first of all, they're probably pretty desperate over there, or if they aren't now, they soon will be. The fact that they're in this part of space at all, instead of wherever it was the Mayor directed them, back when I came on board here, shows that something went wrong with their first job, too."

Anderson snapped a switch on his chair. "Probability?" he said to the surrounding air.

"SEVENTY-TWO PER CENT," the air said back, making Chris start. He still had not gotten used to the idea that the City Fathers overheard everything one said, everywhere and all the time; among many other things, the city was their laboratory in human psychology, which in turn enabled them to answer such questions as Anderson had just asked.

"Well, score another for you," the sergeant said in a troubled voice.

"But I hadn't quite gotten to my point yet, sir. The thing is, now *this* job has gone sour on them too, so they must be awfully low on supplies. No matter how good our strategy is, it has to assume that the other side is going to react logically. But desperate men almost never behave logically; look at German strategy in the last year of World War Two, for instance."

"Never heard of it," Anderson admitted. "But it seems to make sense. What's the other hole?"

"The other one is really only a guess," Chris said. "It's based on what I know about Frank Lutz, and I only saw him twice, and heard one of his aides talk about him. But I don't think he'd ever allow anybody to out-bluff him; he'd always fight first. He has to prove he's the toughest guy in any situation, or his goose is cooked—somebody else'll take over. It's always like that in a thug society—look at the history of the Kingdom of Naples, or Machiavelli's Florence."

"I'm beginning to suspect you're just inventing these examples," Anderson said, frowning blackly. "But again, it does make a certain amount of sense—and nobody but you knows even a little about this man Lutz. Supposing you're right; what could we do about it that we're not doing now?"

"You could use the desperation," Chris said eagerly. "If Lutz and his gang are desperate, then the ordinary citizen must be on the edge of smashing things up. And I'm sure they don't have any 'citizens' in our sense of the word, because the aide I mentioned before let slip that they were short on the drugs. I think he meant me to overhear him, but it didn't mean anything to me at the time. The man on the street must hate the gang even in good times. We could use them to turn Lutz out."

"How?" Anderson said, with the air of a man posing a question he knows to be unanswerable.

"I don't know exactly. It'd have to be done more or less by feel. But I used to have at least two friends over there, one of them with constant access to Lutz. If he's still around and I could sneak over there and get in touch with him—"

Anderson held up a hand and sighed. "I was kind of afraid you were going to trot out something like that. Chris, when are we going to cure you of this urge to go junketing? You know what Amalfi said about that."

"Circumstances alter cases," Carla put in.

"Yes, but—oh, all right, all right, I'll go one step farther, at least." Once more he snapped the switch, and said to the air: "Comments?"

"WE ADVISE AGAINST SUCH A VENTURE, SERGEANT ANDERSON. THE CHANCE THAT MISTER DEFORD WOULD BE RECOGNIZED IS PROHIBITIVELY HIGH."

"There, you see?" Anderson said. "Amalfi would ask them the same question. He ignores their advice more often than not, but in this case what they say is just what he's already decided himself."

"Okay," Chris said, not very much surprised. "It's a pretty fuzzy sort of idea, I'll admit. But it was the only one I had."

"There's a lot to it. I'll tell the Mayor your two points, and suggest that we try to do something to stir up the animals over there. Maybe he'll think of another way of tackling that. Cheer up, Chris; it's a darned good thing you told me all this, so you shouldn't feel bad if a small part of what you said gets rejected. You can't win them all, you know."

"I know," Chris said. "But you can try."

If Amalfi thought of any better idea for "stirring up the animals" in Scranton, Chris did not hear of it; and if he tried it, obviously it had no significant effect. While the city worked, Scranton sat sullenly where it was, ominously silent, while New York's contract termination date drew closer and closer. Poor and starving though it must have been, Scranton had no intention of being outsat at the game of playing for so rich a planet as Argus III; if Amalfi wanted Scranton off the planet, he was going to have to throw it off—or call for the cops. Frank Lutz was behaving pretty much as Chris had predicted, at least so far.

Then, in the last week of the contract, the roof fell in.

Chris got the news, as usual, from his guardian. "It's your friend Piggy," he said wrathfully. "He had the notion that he could pretend to turn his coat, worm his way into Scranton's government, and then pull off some sort of coup. Of course Lutz didn't believe him, and now we're all in the soup."

Chris was torn between shock and laughter. "But how'd he get there?"

"That's one of the worst parts of it. Somehow he sold two women on the idea of being deadly female spies, concubine type, as if a thug government ever had any shortage of women, especially in a famine! One of them

125

is a sixteen-year-old girl whose family is spitting flames, for every good reason. The other is a thirty-year-old passenger who's the sister of a citizen, and *he's* one of Irish Dulany's fighter pilots. The sister, the City Fathers tell us now, is a borderline psychotic, which is why she never made citizenship herself; but they authorized the brother to teach her to fly because it seemed to help her clinically. She stole the boarding-squad plane for the purpose, and by the time we got the whole story from the machines, it was all over."

"You mean that the City Fathers heard Piggy and the others planning all this?"

"Sure they did. They hear everything—you know that."

"But why didn't they tell somebody?" Chris demanded.

"They're under orders never to volunteer information. And a good thing too, almost all the time; without such an order they'd be jabbering away on all channels every minute of the day—they have no judgment. Now Lutz is demanding ransom. We'd pay any reasonable sum, but what he wants is the planet—you were right again, Chris, logic has gone out the window over there —and we can't give him what we don't own, and we wouldn't if we could. Piggy has gotten us into a war, and not even the machines can see what the consequences will be."

Chris blew out his breath in a long gust. "What are we going to do?"

"Can't tell you."

"No, I don't want to know about tactics or anything like that. Just a general idea. Piggy *is* a friend of mine —it sounds silly right now, but I really like him."

"If you don't like a man when he's in trouble, you probably never liked him at all," the perimeter sergeant agreed reflectively. "Well, I can't tell you very much more, all the same. In general terms, Amalfi is stalling in a way he hopes will give Lutz the idea that he's going to give in, but won't give the Argidae the same impression; the machines have run him up a set of key words that should convey the one thing to the colonists and the other to Scranton. Contract termination is only a week away, and if we can stall Lutz until the day before that—well, I can't say what we'll do. But generally, again, we'll move in there and deprive him of his marbles. That'll give us a day to get out of this system before the cops come running, and when they do catch us, at least they'll find that we have a fulfilled contract. Incidentally, it also gives us a day to collect our pay—"

"OVERRIDE," the City Fathers said suddenly, without being asked anything at all.

"Woof! Sorry. Either I've already said one word too many, or I was going to. Can't say anything else, Chris."

"But I though they never volunteered information!"

"They don't," Anderson said. "That wasn't volunteered. They are under orders from Amalfi to monitor talk about this situation and shut it up when it begins to get too loose. That's all I can say—and it's none of it the best news I ever spread."

Only a week to go—and the contract date, Chris realized for the first time, was exactly one day before his birthday. Everything was going to be gained or lost within the same three days: for himself, for Piggy and his two victims, for Scranton, for Argus III, for the city.

And again he knew, as surely as he knew his left hand from his right, that Amalfi's present plan was not going to work.

And again the rock upon which it was sure to founder was Frank Lutz.

Chris did not doubt that Amalfi could outsmart Lutz hands down in any face-to-face situation, but that was not what this was. He did doubt, and doubted most thoroughly, that any list of trigger words the City Fathers could prepare could fool Lutz for long, no matter how well they lulled the hundred eyes of Argus

127

to sleep; the city manager of Scranton was educated, shrewd, experienced in the ways of politics and power—and by now, on top of all that, he would be almost insanely suspicious. Suspicion of everyone had been normal for him even in good times; if he suspected his friends when things were going right, he would hardly be more trustful of his enemies in the very last days of a disaster.

Chris knew very little yet about the politics of Okie cities, but he knew his history. Also, he knew skunks; he had often marveled at the obduracy with which poor Kelly had failed to profit by his tangles with them. Maybe the dog had liked them; they are affectionate pets for a cautious master. But the human variety was not worth the risk. One look at Frank Lutz had taught Chris that.

And even supposing that Lutz did not shoot from the hip while New York was still trying to stall, bringing down upon the city a rain of missiles or whatever other bombardment Scranton was able to mount; even supposing that Lutz was totally taken in by Amalfi's strategy, so that New York took his city away from him at the very last minute, without firing a shot or losing a man; even supposing all this—and it was an impossible budget of suppositions—Piggy and the two women prisoners would not survive it. In New York only Chris could know with what contempt Lutz treated the useless people aboard his own town; and only Chris could guess what short shrift he would give three putative refugees from a great city that did tolerate passengers.

Piggy's pitiful expedition was probably heaving slag right now. If Lutz allowed them to live, more or less, through the next week, he would certainly have them executed the instant he saw his realm toppling, no matter how fast Amalfi moved upon Scranton when the H-hour arrived—it takes no more than five seconds to order that hostages be sacrificed. That was the whole and only reason why the many wars of medieval Earth had gone on so many years after all the participants had forgotten why they had been started or, if they remembered, no longer cared: there was still ransom money to be made.

His guardian was already impatient of that kind of example, however. As for Amalfi and the City Fathers, they had made their position too clear to be worth appealing to now. Were Chris to go back to them, they would give him more than another No; such an approach would give them all the reasons they could possibly need to put Chris under a 24-hour watch.

Yet this time he *knew* they were wrong; and this time he planned very carefully, fighting off the constant conviction that these ancient men and machines could not possibly have made a mistake . . . and would snap the switch on him at any moment.

If they knew what he was up to, they remained inactive, and kept their own counsel. He trudged out of the city the next night. Nobody tried to stop him. Nobody even seemed to see him go.

That was exactly what he had hoped for; but it made him feel miserably in the wrong, and on his own.

11

THE HIDEY HOLE

Ordinarily Chris would not have ventured into a strange wilderness at night; even under present circumstances, he would have left perhaps an hour before sunrise, leaving himself only enough darkness to put distance between himself and any possible pursuit. But on Argus III, he had several advantages going for him.

One of these was a homing compass, a commonplace Okie object the needle of which always pointed toward the strongest nearby spindizzy field. On most plants, cities tended to keep a fractional field going to prevent the local air from mixing with that of the city itself—and when the city was on a war footing, the generators would be kept running as a matter of course, in case a quick getaway should be needed. The gadget would point him away from New York for half his trip, and an ordinary magnetic compass would serve to show which way; thereafter, the homing compass would be pointing steadily toward Scranton.

The second advantage was light. Argus had no moon —but it had the hundred eyes of the nearby blue-white giant suns of the cluster, and beyond them the diffuse light of the rest of the cluster, throughout this half of the year. The aggregate sky glow was almost twice as bright as Earthly moonlight—more than good enough to read by, and to cast sharp shadows, though not quite enough to trigger the color sensitivity of the human eye.

Most important of all, Chris knew pine woods and mountains. He had grown up among them.

He traveled light, carrying with him only a small pack containing two tins of field rations, a canteen and a change of clothing. The "fresh" clothes were those he had been wearing when he had first been transferred to New York; it had taken considerable courage to ask the City Fathers if they were still in storage, despite his knowledge that the machines never told what they knew unless asked. The request left behind a clue, but that really didn't matter; once Sgt. Anderson realized Chris was missing, he could be in little doubt about where he had gone.

By dawn he was almost over the crest of the range. By noon he had found himself a cave on the other side from which a small, ice-cold stream issued. He went very cautiously into this, as deep as he could go on his hands and knees, looking for old bones, droppings, bedding or any other sign that some local animal lived there. He found none, as he had expected; few animals care to make a home directly beside running water—it is too damp at night, and it attracts too many potential enemies. Then he ate for the first time and went to sleep.

He awoke at dusk, refilled his canteen from the stream, and began the long scramble down the other side of the range. The route he took was necessarily more than a little devious, but thanks to the two compasses he was never in any doubt about his bearings for more than a few minutes at a time. Long before midnight, he caught his first glimpse of Scranton, glowing dully in the valley like a scatter of dewdrops in a spider's web. By dawn, he had buried his pack along with the New York clothes —by now more than a little dirty and torn—and was shambling cheerfully across the cleared perimeter of Scranton, toward the same street by which he had boarded the town willy-nilly so long ago. There were many differences this time, not the least of which was his possession of the necessary device for getting through the edge of the spindizzy field.

He was spotted at once, of course, and two guards came trotting out to meet him, red-eyed and yawning; obviously, it was near the end of their trick.

"Whatcha doin' out here?"

"Went to pick mushrooms," Chris said, with what he hoped was an idiotic grin. "Didn't find any. Funny kind of woods they got here."

One of the sleepy guards looked him over, but apparently saw nothing but the issue clothing and Chris's obvious youth. He cussed Chris out more or less routinely and said:

"Where ya work?"

"Soaking pits."

The two guards exchanged glances. The soaking pits were deep, electrically heated holes in which steel ingots were cooled, gently and slowly. Occasionally they had to be cleaned, but it wasn't economical to turn the heat off. The men who did the job were lowered into the pits in asbestos suits for four minutes at a time, which was the period it took for their insulating wooden shoes to burst into flame; then they were hauled out, given new shoes, and lowered into the pit again—and this went on for a full working day. Nobody but the mentally deficient could safely be assigned to such an inferno.

"Awright, feeb, get back on the job. And don't come out here no more, get me? You're lucky we didn't shoot you."

Chris ducked his head, grinned, and ran. A minute later, he was twisting and dodging through the shabby streets. Despite his confidence, he was a little surprised at how well he remembered them.

The hidey hole among the crates was still there, too, exactly as he and Frad had last left it, even to the stub of candle. Chris ate his other tin of field rations, and sat down in the darkness to wait.

He did not have to wait long, though the time *seemed* endless. About an hour after the end of the work day, he heard the sounds of someone threading the labyrinth with sure steps; and then the light of the flash came darting in upon him.

"Hi, Frad," he said. "I'm glad to see you. Or I will be, once you get that light out of my eyes."

The spoor of the flashlight beam swung toward the ceiling. "Is that you, Chris?" Frad's voice said. "Yep, I see it is. But you must have grown a foot."

"I guess I have. I'm sorry I didn't get here sooner."

The big man sat down with a grunt. "Never thought you'd make it at all—it was just a hunch, once I heard who it was we were up against. I hope you're not trying to switch sides, like those other three idiots."

"Are they still alive?" Chris said with sudden fear.

"Yep. As of an hour ago. But I wouldn't put any money on them lasting. Frank is getting wilder by the day—I used to think I understood him, but not any more. Is that what you're here for—to try and sneak those kids out? You can't do it."

"No," Chris said. "Or anyhow, not exactly. And I'm not trying to switch sides, either. But we were wondering why you let your city manager get you into this mess. Our City Fathers say he's gone off his rocker, and if the machines can see it, you ought to be able to. In fact, you just said you did."

"I've heard about those machines of yours," Frad said slowly. "Do they really run the city, the way the stories say?"

"They run most of it. They don't boss it, though; the Mayor does that."

"Amalfi. Hmm. To tell you the truth, Chris, everybody knows that Frank's lost control. But there's nothing we can do about it. Suppose we threw him out—not that it'd be easy—where'd we go from there? We'd still be in the same mess."

"You wouldn't be at war with my town any more," Chris suggested.

"No, and that'd be a gain, as far as it went. But we'd still be in the rest of the hole. Just changing a set of names won't put any money in the till, or any bread in our mouths." He paused for a moment and then added bitterly, "I suppose you know we're starving. Not me, personally—Frank feeds his own—but I don't eat very well either when I have to look at the faces I meet on the streets. Frank's big play against Amalfi is crazy, sure—but except for that we've got *no* hope."

Chris was silent. It was what he had expected to find, but that made the problem no easier.

"But you haven't answered my question," Frad said. "What are you up to? Just collecting information? Maybe I should have kept my mouth shut."

"I'm trying to promote a revolution," Chris said. It sounded embarrassingly pompous, but he couldn't think of any other way to put it. He was also trying to avoid saying anything which would be an outright lie, but from this point onward that was going to be increasingly difficult. "The Mayor says you must have flunked your contracts because you don't have any machines to judge them. Evidently that happens a lot of times to small cities that don't have computer control. And the City Fathers say you *could* have done this job."

"Now wait a minute. Let's take this one step at a time. Suppose we got rid of Frank and patched things up with Amalfi. Could we get some help from your City Fathers on reorganizing the job?"

Now the guesswork had to begin, to be followed rapidly by the outright lying. "Sure you could. But we'd have to have our people back first—Piggy Kingston-Throop and the two women."

Frad made a quick gesture of dismissal in the dim light. "I'd do that for a starter, not as part of a deal. But look, Chris, this is a complicated business. Your city landed here to do the job we defaulted on. If we do it after all, then somebody doesn't get paid. Not a likely deal for Amalfi to make."

"Mayor Amalfi isn't offering any deal yet. But Frad, you know what our contract with Argus is like. Half of it is to do the job you didn't do, sure. But the other half of it is to get rid of Scranton. If you turn into a decent town instead of a bindlestiff, we'll get that part of the money—and it's the bigger part, now. Naturally the Mayor'd rather do it by finagling than by fighting—if we fight, we'll need all the money and more just to pay for the damages, both of us. Isn't that logical?"

"Hmm. I guess it is. But if you want to keep *me* reasonable, you'd better lay off that word 'bindlestiff.' It's true enough, but it makes me mad all the same. Either we treat as equals, or we don't treat."

"I'm sorry," Chris said. "I don't know a lot about this kind of thing. The Mayor would have sent somebody else if he'd had anybody who could have gotten in. But there wasn't anyone but me."

"Okay. I'm edgy, that's all. But there's one thing more, and that's the colonists. They're not going to trust us just because we've gotten rid of Frank. *They* don't know that he's the problem, and they'll have no better reason to trust the next city manager. If we're going to get back the mining part of the contract, Amalfi will have to guarantee it. Would he do that?"

Chris was already in far deeper waters than his conscience could possibly justify. He knew abruptly that he could push no farther into the untrue and the unknown.

"I don't know, Frad. I never asked, and he didn't say. I suppose he'd have to ask the City Fathers for an opinion first—and *nobody* knows what they might say."

Frad squatted and thought about it, smacking one fist repeatedly into the other palm. After a moment, he seemed about to ask another question, but it never got out.

"Well," he muttered finally, "every deal has one carrot in it. I guess we take the chance. You'll have to stay here, Chris. I can knock Barney's and Huggins' heads together easy enough, but Frank's something else again. When the shooting really starts, he might turn out to be a lot faster than I am—and besides, he won't care what else he hits. If I manage to dump him I'll come back for you soon enough—but you'd better stay out of sight until it's over."

Chris had expected nothing else, but the prospect of again missing all the excitement, while he simply sat and waited, disappointed him all the same. However, it also reminded him of something.

"I'll stay here. But, Frad, if it doesn't look as if it's working, don't wait till it's hopeless. Let me know and I'll try to get help."

"Well . . . all right. But better not to have any outsiders visible if it's going to stick. If anybody in this town sees New York's finger in this, even people who hate Frank'll be on his side again. We're all a little crazy around here lately."

He stood up, his face somber, and picked up the flashlight.

"I hope you've got the straight goods," he said. "I don't like to do this. Frank trusts me—I guess I'm the last man he does trust. And for some reason I always liked him, even though I knew he was a louse from the very beginning. Some guys hit you that way. It's not going to be fun, stabbing him in the back. He's got it coming, sure—but all the same I wouldn't do it if I didn't trust you more."

He swung to the exit into the labyrinth. Chris swallowed and said: "Thanks, Frad. Good luck."

"Sit tight. I'll see you."

Of necessity, Chris did not stay in the hole every minute of the day, but even so he found that he quickly lost track of the passage of time. He ate when he seemed to need to—though most of the food had been removed from the hide-out, Frad had missed one compact cache —and slept as much as possible. That was not very much, however, for now that he was inactive he found himself a prey to more and more anxiety and tension, made worse by his total ignorance of what was going on outside.

Finally he was convinced that the deadline had passed. After this, all possibility of sleep vanished; from minute to minute he awaited the noises of battle joined, or the deepening drone which would mean that Scranton was carrying him off again. The close confines of the hole made the tension even more nightmarish. At the first faint sound in the labyrinth, he jumped convulsively, and would have started like a hare had there been any place to run to.

In the uncertain light of the flash, Frad looked ghastly: he had several days' growth of beard and was haggard with sleeplessness. In addition, he had a beautiful black eye.

"Come on out," he said tersely. "The job's mostly done."

Chris followed Frad out into the half-light of the warehouse, which seemed brilliant after the stuffy inkiness of the hole, and thence into the intolerable brilliance of late-afternoon sunlight.

"What happened to Frank Lutz?" he said breathlessly.

Frad stared straight ahead, and when he replied, his voice was totally devoid of expression.

"We got rid of him. The subject is closed."

Chris shied off from it hastily. "What happens now?"

"There's still a little mopping up to do, and we could

use some help. If you called your friends now, we could let them in—as long as Amalfi doesn't send a whole boarding squad."

"No, just two men."

Frad nodded. "Two good men in full armor should flatten things out in a day or so at the most." He hailed a passing Tin Cab. As it settled obediently beside them, Chris saw that there were several inarguable bullet holes in it. How old they were was of course impossible to know, but it was Chris's guess that they hadn't been there for as much as a week. "I'll get you to the radio and you can take it from there. Then it'll be time to get the deal drawn up."

And that would be the moment that Chris had been dreading above all others—the moment when he would have to talk to Anderson and Amalfi, and tell them what he had done, what he had started, what he had committed them to.

There was no doubt in his mind as to how he felt about it. He was scared.

"Come on, hop in," Frad said. "What are you waiting for?"

12

AN INTERVIEW WITH AMALFI

The city was still administered, with due regard for tradition, from City Hall, but its control room was in the mast of the Empire State Building. It was here that Amalfi received them all—Chris, Frad, and Sgts. Anderson and Dulany—for he had been occupying it around the clock while the alert had been on, as officially it still was.

It was a marvelous place, jammed to the ceilings with screens, lights, meters, automatic charts, and scores of devices Chris could not even put a name to; but Chris was more interested in the Mayor. Since he was at the moment talking to Frad, Chris had plenty of opportunity to study him.

The fabulous Amalfi had turned out to be a complete surprise. Chris could not say any more just what kind of man he had pictured in his mind. Something more stalwart, lean and conventionally heroic, perhaps—but certainly not a short barrel-shaped man with a bull neck, a totally bald head and hands so huge that they looked as though they could crush rocks. The oddest touch of all was the cigar, held in the powerful fingers with almost feminine delicacy, and drawn on with invariable relish. Nobody else in the city smoked—*nobody* else—because there was no place in it to grow tobacco. The cigar, then, was more than a badge of office; it was a symbol of the wealth of the city, like the snow imported from the mountains by the Roman emperors, and Amalfi treated it like a treasure, not a habit. When he was thinking, he had an odd way of holding it up and looking at it, as though everything that was going on in his head was concentrated in its glowing coal.

He was saying to Frad: "The arrangements with the machinery is cumbersome, but not difficult in principle. We can lend you our Brood assembly until she replicates herself; then you reset the daughter machine, feed her scrap, and out come City Fathers to the number that you'll need—probably about a third as many as we carry, and it'll take maybe ten years. You can use the time feeding them data, because in the beginning they'll be idiots except for the computation function.

"In the meantime we'll refigure your job problem on our own machines. Since we'll trust the answer, and since Chris says you're a man of your word, that means that of course we'll underwrite your contract with the Argidae."

"Many thanks," Frad said.

"Not necessary," Amalfi rumbled. "For value received. In fact we got more than we're paying for—we learned something from you. Which brings us to our drastic friend Mr. deFord." He swung on Chris, who tried unsuccessfully to swallow his heart. "I suppose you're aware, Chris, that this is D-day for you: your eighteenth birthday."

"Yes, sir. I sure am."

"Well, I've got a job for you if you want it. I've been studying it ever since it was first mentioned to me, and all I can say is, it serves you right."

Chris swallowed again. The Mayor studied the cigar judiciously.

"It calls for a very odd combination of skills and character traits. Taking the latter first, it needs initiative,

140

boldness, imagination, a willingness to improvise and take short-cuts, and an ability to see the whole of a complex situation at a glance. But at the same time, it needs conservative instincts, so that even the boldest ideas and acts tend to be those that save men, materials, time, money. What class of jobs does that make you think of so far?"

"MILITARY GENERAL OFFICERS," the City Fathers promptly announced.

"I wasn't talking to you," Amalfi growled. He was plainly irritated, but it seemed to Chris an old irritation, almost a routine one. "Chris?"

"Well, sir, they're right, of course. I might even have thought of it myself, though I can't swear to it. At least all the great generals follow that pattern."

"Okay. As for the skills, a lot of them are required, but only one is cardinal. The man has got to be a first-class cultural morphologist."

Chris recognized the term, from his force feeding in Spengler. It denoted a scholar who could look at any culture at any stage in its development, relate it to all other cultures at similar stages, and come up with specific predictions of how these people would react to a given proposal or event. It surely wouldn't be a skill a general would ever be likely to have a use for, even if he had the time to develop it.

"You've got the character traits, that's plain to see—including the predisposition toward the skill. Most Okies have that, but in nowhere near the degree you seem to. The skill itself, of course, can only emerge with time and practice . . . but you'll have lots of time. The City Fathers say five years' probation.

"As for the city, we never had such a job on the roster before, but a study of Scranton and some more successful towns convinces us that we need it. Will you take it?"

Chris's head was whirling with a wild, humming mixture of pride and bafflement. "Excuse me, Mr. Mayor—but just what is it?"

"City manager."

Chris stared at Sgt. Anderson, but his guardian looked as stunned as Chris felt. After a moment, however, he winked solemnly. Chris could not speak; but at last he managed to nod his head. It was all the management he was capable of, right now.

"Good. The City Fathers predicted you would, so you were started on the drugs in your first meal of today. Welcome to citizenship, Mr. deFord."

Even at this moment, however, a part of Chris's mind seemed curiously detached. He was thinking of the original reason he had wanted long life: in the hope that some day, somehow, he might yet get back home. It had never occurred to him that by the time that happened, there would be nothing left back there that he could call his own. Even now, Earth was unthinkably remote, not only in space, but in his heart.

His definition of "home" had changed. He had won long life; but with it, new ties and new obligations; not an eternal childhood on Earth, but a life for the stars.

He wrenched his attention back to the control room. "What about Piggy?" he said curiously. "I talked to him on the way back. He seems to have learned a lot."

"Too late," Amalfii said, his voice inflexibly stern. "He wrote his own ticket. It's a passenger ticket. He's got boldness and initiative, all right—all of it of the wrong kind, totally untempered by judgment or imagination. The same kind of pitfall will always lie ahead of you, Chris; that, too, is an aspect of the job. It'd be wise not to forget it."

Chris nodded again, but the warning could not dampen his spirits now; for this was for some reason the highest moment of them all—the moment when Frad

Haskins, the new city manager of Scranton, shook his hand and said huskily:

"Colleague, let's talk business."

Author's Note

The future society of nomad cities which serves as the background for this story is also the subject of three more books. These were intended primarily for older readers, but *A Life for the Stars* is, I hope a sufficient key to admit anyone into the world of the interstellar wanderers.

Together, the four books tell a connected history, and I've listed them here in their proper order, rather than the order in which they were published. The first is called *They Shall Have Stars*. It takes place in the very near future, and shows how the discoveries which made the nomad cities possible came about. Thus it's a sort of prologue, and it's rather short, as a proper prologue should be.

All the rest of the books show the nomad cities in action. The next in the series is the one you have just read. The third, which is called *Earthman, Come Home*, carries the history from about A.D. 3600 to about 3950, and so is by far the longest of the four. Finally, there is *The Triumph of Time*, which covers the relatively brief span of time from the end of *Earthman* to A.D. 4004.

Despite all these centuries, though, you'll find that the last two books contain several people whom you've met for the first time in these pages. To live so long a life would certainly be remarkable, but it would be more than a gift or a miracle; it would be a privilege. *A Life for the Stars* tells how that privilege might be earned.

JAMES BLISH